SPY GEAR ADVENTURES

BOOK 5

THE SHRIEKING SHADOW

To Big Guy,
I hope you
like the
Books!
Love,
Dad

READ ALL THE
SPYGEAR
ADVENTURES

SPY GEAR

BOOK 5

ADVENTURES

THE SHRIEKING SHADOW

BY RICK BARBA

ALADDIN PAPERBACKS
New York London Toronto Sydney

ALADDIN PAPERBACKS
An imprint of Simon & Schuster Children's Publishing Division
1230 Avenue of the Americas, New York, NY 10020
Text copyright © 2007 by Wild Planet Entertainment, Inc.
Illustrations copyright © 2006 by Scott M. Fischer
Map of Carrolton copyright © 2006 by Eve Steccati
All rights reserved. Spy Gear and Wild Planet trademarks
are the property of Wild Planet Entertainment, Inc.
San Francisco, CA 94104
All rights reserved, including the right of reproduction
in whole or in part in any form.
ALADDIN PAPERBACKS and colophon are
trademarks of Simon & Schuster, Inc.
Designed by Tom Daly
The text of this book was set in Weiss.
Manufactured in the United States of America
First Aladdin Paperbacks edition March 2007
2 4 6 8 10 9 7 5 3 1
Library of Congress Control Number 2006940044
ISBN-13: 978-1-4169-0891-3
ISBN-10: 1-4169-0891-9

CONTENTS

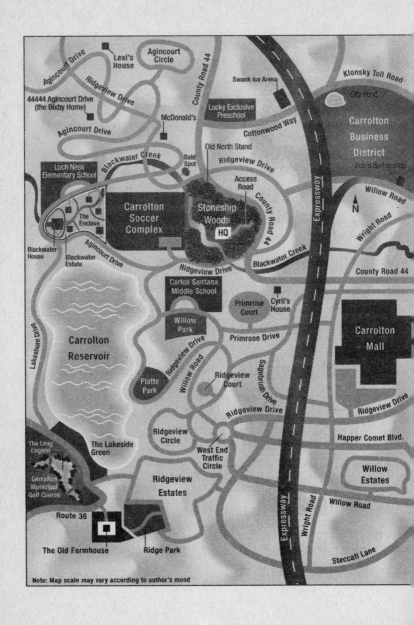

Note: Map scale may vary according to author's mood

TEAM SPY GEAR

 JAKE BIXBY

 LUCAS BIXBY

 CYRIL WONG

 LEXI LOPEZ

ANTS OR NOT?

Spring has sprung into Carrolton like . . . oh, like *a madman crazed with insanity*! Okay, maybe that's a lame metaphor. But I can't help it! Life is exploding everywhere! After the frigid lockdown of Carrolton's brutal winter, the sight of green tree buds makes everyone in town go wacky with wackiness.

Just look at them down there.

Oh. Please zoom in your spy satellite photo lens to a magnification x600.

Good. Now focus in on that big green square covered with white rectangles. That's the Carrolton Soccer Complex. It's big . . . so big that it's one of only eight hundred suburban soccer complexes that can be seen with the naked eye from my office window on the International Space Station.

If you zoom in another x30 or so, you see that these particular soccer fields are covered with ants. Wait! Those are kids, not ants. Sorry.

Yes, it's Saturday in spring, and that means soccer! See the hundreds of kids waving their feelers in the air, clamping their huge jaws around crumbs that look like boulders, and then digging in all eight legs as they haul the massive food-chunk back to the hive and wait a minute, those are actually ants. Apparently, you zoomed in too far. (This seems to happen to us at least once every book, doesn't it?)

But no, these aren't ants. Ants have six legs, not eight. What are these things?

Spiders, maybe? Spiders have eight legs, right?

But these don't look or act like spiders. Spiders are solitary; they don't swarm like this.

Interesting.

Okay, well, let's move on, shall we? This isn't the Discovery Channel, after all.

Zoom out now.

Ah, there we go. Over there, on the grass.

See? *Those* are kids. Soccer kids. Hundreds of them. Thousands, maybe.

Of course, not *every* kid in Carrolton is playing soccer at this exact moment. No, some kids played their games earlier. Others will play later. And, shockingly, six Carrolton kids don't play soccer at all. We think they're Commies.[1]

Let's go find the Bixbys.

Pan your spycam northwest from the Soccer Complex, across Agincourt Drive, across Blackwater Creek, across Agincourt Drive again, then across Agincourt Drive again. See that gray house, the colonial at 44444 Agincourt Drive? That's the Bixby house.

Now peer into the windows and violate their privacy, like a good spy.

Hmmm, nobody's home.

Let's scan around the neighborhood a bit. Maybe the Bixbys are taking a walk.

Yes, the Bixbys often take family walks after soccer on Saturdays. They must be around here someplace. Just follow the streets . . . *ha*! That was a joke. To "follow the streets" in Carrolton you need the iron gut of an astronaut. Indeed, streets in the Bixby neighborhood have more twists and turns than the Cookie Woofer, a truly sick roller coaster at Forty Mounds of Fun, the theme park and vomitorium just north of the business district. Okay, it's not really a vomitorium; it's just a theme park. But people uneat their lunch on rides at Forty Mounds of Fun all the time because these rides are so insanely crazy and wacky and mad. Say, how did we get to this fun

1. Kids, you'll have to ask your parents about Commies. They used to be everywhere.

3

topic of yorking meaty chunks on rides? Oh, right, we were looking for the Bixbys.

Scan around again. Follow the sidewalks. Slowly.

While you're at it, check out those lawns. Don't they look healthy?

That's because they actually *are* healthy.

See, unlike in other towns, where people nuke their weeds with industrial poisons and then scatter other chemicals all over the grass to help it "grow" (actually, the grass mutates into drug-addicted green tentacles), folks in Carrolton generally use organic and poison-free methods of gardening and lawn care. I say "generally" because there are exceptions. Every once in a while, some fool tries to lay down a patch of poison to kill some poor species of plant that never did anything wrong other than fail to be Kentucky bluegrass.

But then that neighbor gets to meet Dr. Tim.

When I say "meet Dr. Tim," I say it loudly with quotation marks around it.

Because if you're spraying common garden poisons on your lawn anywhere in Dr. Tim's neighborhood, which is the Bixbys' neighborhood too, the way you "meet" Dr. Tim is by running in terror as he chases you with a Bolivian machete.

Dr. Tim has a PhD and is a scientist who left a well-paid, high-level position at a government laboratory called

NCAR (National Center for Atmospheric Research) to start a lawn service. That may sound like an odd choice, but back then, Dr. Tim was so angry about his research into pesticides (poisons that kill bugs) and herbicides (poisons that kill weeds) that he decided to start a company, which he calls Native Care Solutions Inc.

Now Dr. Tim provides organic, nonpoisonous ways to control bugs and weeds that invade your home or lawn. His motto is: "If it's green and soft, there's a place for it in my yard."

Thus Dr. Tim has also become the neighborhood lawn cop. He angrily patrols the streets, on the lookout for poison usage. People fear him. It doesn't help that Dr. Tim also *looks* insane, with his torn gaucho hat resting above huge, bushy white eyebrows. His wild, white mustache and piercing blue eyes give people the notion that he's a madman capable of unspeakable mayhem.

Uh-oh, looks like we're about to get a demonstration.

See that guy over there? That's Ted Barky. He's new in town.

Note how Ted sprays that yellow hissing liquid onto the dandelions by his sidewalk.

Do you hear that? That little squeaking sound?

That's the sound of dandelions shrieking in agony.

Note the product name on Ted's spray bottle: WEED-SLAUGHTER PLUS.

How bad is the stuff? This bad: When Ted shakes the

bottle, insane laughter can be heard. It comes from inside the bottle.

Note also how neighbors up and down Agincourt Drive stare in utter disbelief at Ted Barky. Some start edging toward their houses. Then a big white pickup truck rolls slowly around the corner; the neighbors drop their gardening tools and hurry inside. Doors slam up and down the street.

But poor Ted doesn't notice.

He just keeps spraying the smoking, fizzling, bubbling yellow liquid onto his lawn.

The white pickup truck stops next to Ted, and Dr. Tim steps out. Ted glances up, nods in a neighborly way, and keeps slaying weeds with lethal toxins. Then he suddenly halts the slaughter. He frowns and crouches low, staring at something on the ground.

Dr. Tim approaches. Eyes aglow with mad intensity, he gazes at Ted and says, "You're new."

Ted Barky glances up at Dr. Tim. "Yes, we just moved in two weeks ago. Are you a neighbor?"

"Yes. Yes, I am." Dr. Tim points up the street toward his house.

"I'm Ted Barky," says Ted Barky.

"I'm Dr. Tim."

"Hey, Tim."

"Hello," says Dr. Tim loudly. "I'm wondering, Ted, what is that yellow stuff there?"

"Weed killer," says Ted, still staring at the ground.

"Weed killer," repeats Dr. Tim. His smile looks like a grimace of searing pain.

"Yes," says Ted. "I use it to kill weeds."

"Do you mind if I . . . look at the bottle, Ted?" If you knew Dr. Tim like I do, you'd know that he is struggling right now to keep from sprouting fangs to sink into Ted Barky's throat.

"Why?" asks Ted, glancing up again.

"I want to scan the ingredients," says Dr. Tim. "I'm a scientist, Ted."

"Really?" Ted hands the Weed-Slaughter Plus spray bottle to Dr. Tim. "Say, Tim, do you know anything about ants?"

Dr. Tim takes a deep breath. Then he says, "Ted, I know *everything* about ants."

"Look at these guys," says Ted, pointing at the edge of his lawn. "Check out that anthill."

Dr. Tim crouches, and jabs his nose inches from the grass. "Those aren't ants," he says.

"They're not?" says Ted, puzzled.

Dr. Tim frowns. "No, they're not," he says. Then he does something very unusual. He sets down the bottle of deadly lawn poison and forgets about it. If you knew Dr. Tim like I do, you'd realize that we'd all better pay close mind to whatever has grabbed Dr. Tim's attention at this moment.

Ted Barky says, "If they're not ants, then what are they?"

Dr. Tim looks puzzled. "I don't know."

"They look like ants."

Dr. Tim nods. "But ants have six legs," he says. "These have eight."

"Maybe they're spiders," says Ted.

"Spiders don't have three body segments or live in communal hives," says Dr. Tim. "These do."

(Say, doesn't this sound familiar?)

"Well, they look like ants," says Ted.

"But they're not," says Dr. Tim.

"Then what are they?"

"I don't know."

Dr. Tim thrusts his hand into his pants pocket and yanks out a tiny plastic tube with a screened lid. He uncaps the tube, scoops up several of the odd insects— maybe nine or ten of them, plus a bit of their hive—and then pops the lid back on.

Then he turns and glares deeply into Ted Barky's eyes.

Ted faints.

Grinning, Dr. Tim trudges back to his pickup truck. He doesn't mind scaring people if it means fewer poisons in our environment. As Tim trudges, he glances at the specimen tube. Then he stops.

He frowns, staring at the tube.

Where there had been a dozen antlike insects, now there's only one.

And it's huge.

2

BUBBLES IN THE LAGOON

Okay, this is getting ridiculous. Where in East Halibut are the Bixbys?

Did Viper abduct them?

Let's keep looking.

Pan down to the Carrolton Reservoir, that big blue body of water to the south.

Isn't it beautiful?

See all the people over there on the Lakeside Green, the big, grassy area along the southeast shore? Dozens of blankets are spread out, picnics left and right. Frisbees and footballs fly, kids laugh and play tag, parents drink thermos coffee and read the newspaper or just watch their children play.

Wow! The grass is so emerald green, you need a jeweler's eyepiece just to look at it.

And note all the boats out on the water.

Check out that sailboat with the big yellow spinnaker sail. See how it glides over the light chop? I love that. Watch how it leans with the wind and . . .

Wait! *Did you see that?*

Surely you did.

No?

Hmmm. I could have sworn I saw something massively big in the water. Are you sure you didn't see that big shadow moving just under the surface?

It was moving pretty fast.

Okay. Maybe not.

Well, that's the deal about water, especially big water like the Carrolton Reservoir. *Anything* could be swimming in there: sharks, squids, whatever. Well, not in a freshwater lake, of course. I mean, *heh*, you wouldn't see scary saltwater ocean creatures in a reservoir . . . would you? No. Of course not. Something really big or dangerous in a freshwater reservoir would be unusual. Maybe one of a kind. A freak.

Whatever. I don't know why I'm bringing that up.

So, anyway, let's pan back over to the lakeside park. Center your satcam view on that huge red blanket . . . there, that one, the one made from nonallergenic natural fibers woven in Costa Rica by indigenous fair-trade company workers using native-tooled whalebone knitting needles. That red blanket, as you may have guessed, is the blanket of Mrs. Bixby, mother of Jake and Lucas Bixby, the famous spies. See that woman sitting on the blanket? The lady with short, very dark hair? That's her . . . Mrs. Bixby.

Zoom in. She looks relaxed, doesn't she?

Don't be fooled. Mrs. Bixby is never "relaxed."

She is a very busy woman. There is always something to do or worry about or pick up or fold. It's bad enough that she has her own children's welfare to consider, like, every waking minute. But Mrs. Bixby is a school counselor. She has to worry about everybody else's children as well.

Today, as Mrs. Bixby sits on her red blanket making lists the length of Chile in her daily planner, she is *almost* relaxed. As she sips papaya nectar on this sunny, gorgeous afternoon, her boys and husband happily kick a soccer ball nearby. She plans to join them just as soon as she finishes a couple more lists. What could be better than that?

Before she finishes her current list, however, her husband collapses next to her, breathing heavily. That's him: the tall, athletic-looking, blond fellow with corporate business on his mind.

"Tired?" asks Mrs. Bixby.

"I'm old," pants Mr. Bixby.

"You are not."

"Yes, I am."

Mr. Bixby points at his boys, who chase their soccer ball across Route 36, a two-lane country road that curves around the Carrolton Municipal Golf Course to the southwest and then runs along the inland edge of the Lakeside Green.

"See?" he says. "They're young."

"Good lord," says Mrs. Bixby, holding her cheeks in her hands. "They are!"

"Don't mock me." He glances at the daily planner in her lap. The date Mrs. Bixby is planning is three years in the future.

Well, we finally found the Bixbys.

Those of you familiar with the Spy Gear Adventure series need no introduction to these fine Bixby boys. Those of you *un*familiar with the Spy Gear Adventure series have some reading to do, given that Jake and Lucas Bixby have already saved the world four times, and, as an inhabitant of Earth,[2] you are obligated by United Nations Resolution 1057 to read about these world-saving exploits in Spy Gear Adventure Books 1 through 4.

If you don't, you face sanctions, possibly an oil embargo.

Believe me, your economy will suffer.

The taller one there—the thin lad with short brown hair, brown eyes, and a baseball cap turned backward so

2. If you're not an Earthling, please put down this book and report to the spore-mining complex on Xenar 3.

he can snap a good head ball if necessary—is Jake Bixby. He looks unremarkable, a normal kid, just like any kid in a crowd. You wouldn't single him out and say, "Wow, look at that kid." You might even just ignore Jake. But that would be a foolish mistake. Sure, he's a heck of a good kid, that Jake. Everybody likes him, except of course the bad guys. They wish he would go off to college so they could disrupt the world in peace. Unfortunately for them, Jake is only thirteen.

And then there's Lucas. He has so much energy that when you describe him, you have to duck. The key word here is "gusto." His curiosity about how stuff works is legendary. I'm pretty sure Lucas will be either a scientist or an inventor someday.[3] Lucas wears glasses now—he just got them in April—and his hair is so dark, it's almost black, just like his mother's. He also inherited much of his mother's intensity about organizing things. If you ever attend one of Team Spy Gear's operational planning sessions, you'll see what I mean. Lucas is eleven.

The soccer ball rolls to a halt on the far side of Route 36.

Jake Bixby reaches it, nimbly flicks it upward with his right foot, and catches it with his hands. Then he stares at something nearby.

"What the donkey's hoof is that?" he asks, pointing

3. I'll let you know when I decide which.

onto the golf course where, a good fifty yards away, one of the taller, spindlier shrubs is floating down the fairway. No, wait . . . that's not a shrub. It's a mop. Actually, no, it's not a mop, either.

"That's Cyril!" exclaims Jake.

Lucas steps up next to his brother.

"Who, that guy?" he says. "No way! See, he's carrying a golf bag."

"Right," agrees Jake. "That couldn't be Cyril."

The hairy golfer stops and pulls a club out of his bag. He drops the bag, seizes the club with both hands, and starts hacking gruesomely at something in the tall grass of the left rough.

"He's killing something," says Lucas suspiciously.

"My god, that's heinous," says Jake.

Now the golfer lifts the club high over his head, pauses, and takes a huge, violent swing. The momentum twists his upper body so wildly that his hips lock and his legs buckle. The club's arc continues all the way around in a complete circle. As the club swings upward, the golfer's legs splay out at impossible angles and he collapses into a pile of dislocated limbs.

"You're right," says Lucas. "That *is* Cyril."

Jake grins. "And look who's with him."

A dark-haired girl in glasses slogs up beside Cyril, who thrashes about like a rubbery squid-man on the ground. She carries a golf bag too. The girl gazes down

14

at Cyril for a minute, then reaches down and gives him a hand, yanking him back onto his feet.

"It's Cat!" says Lucas.

Jake grins again . . . this time mischievously. Hey, a Bixby knows a good opportunity when he sees it. He drops low and scrambles to a bush near the chain-link fence enclosing the golf course.

"Come on, broseph," he calls back to Lucas, grinning wildly. "Let's *spy* on them!"

Okay, time for a quick primer for new readers who haven't read any previous Spy Gear Adventures. Wait! First, let me mock you.

Okay, that was satisfying.

Now the quick primer:

Cyril Wong is Jake Bixby's best friend. Like Jake, Cyril is thirteen and is an eighth grader at Carlos Santana Middle School. He has a weekly weblog, or blog, that you can actually visit online at www.cyrilsblog.com, if you want to read something really incredibly strange. Cyril is a grim, serious kid who hates squids.

Cat Horton is Cyril's girlfriend, sort of . . . actually, Cyril refers to her as his "friend-girl." She just turned thirteen and is currently a seventh grader at Santana. Cat is very clever, and sometimes helps Team Spy Gear complete their top-secret missions. Her real name is Marmoset, which of course is why everyone calls her "Cat" for short.

So there they are: the Bixbys, Cyril, and Cat.

What a cheery scene! The only important Spy Gear people missing now are Lexi Lopez and Marco and Viper and Mr. Latimer and Mrs. Burnskid and the Dark Man and Halle Berry and Spider-Man, all of whom make frequent appearances in the Spy Gear Adventure series.

Okay, maybe not the last two, but I'll do anything to get you to read Books 1, 2, 3, and 4 so I don't have to introduce everybody and everything in every flipping new Spy Gear book.

I'm getting mad!

Lucas Bixby immediately "goes electronic" on the situation, something he often does. He whips out a pair of Micro Agent Listeners, tosses one to Jake, and jabs his unit's earpiece into his ear.

Both boys listen in to the conversation. But to make things easier for you, we'll move the camera over by Cyril and Cat. Just remember that the Bixbys are listening to everything.

Cyril shades his eyes as he gazes up the fairway toward the tee box.

"Was that a good golf?" he asks Cat. "I didn't see where it went. Did I golf it okay? Was it acceptable golfage?"

"Not quite," replies Cat.

"Why not?" asks Cyril.

"Well, Cyril, you missed the ball," says Cat. "See?" She points at the ground. "There it is."

"That's my golf ball?" asks Cyril. "It looks so *small*."

"Yes," says Cat patiently. "Plus, you were hitting back toward the tee, back where we started this hole, oh, about two hours ago."

"I was?"

"Yes," says Cat. She takes a deep breath. "Remember how I told you about hitting toward the *flag*?" She points down the fairway toward the distant green. "See it way down there?"

Cyril nods, looking. "That's miles away."

Cat drops her own golf bag.

"Let's rest," she says.

Cyril nods his hair vigorously. "I'm exhausted," he says. "It's been a long day." Both kids sit on the fairway grass. "Say, when does golf end? Like, what's our time limit?"

"You play eighteen holes," says Cat.

Cyril looks horrified. "They make you do this *eighteen times*?" He stands up again. "But what if your timer runs out?"

"There is no timer, Cyril," says Cat. "You keep playing until you're finished." She looks up at the sky. "Or, in our case, until darkness falls."

"Dang!" says Cyril, centering his club over the ball again. "Let's golf!"

Cyril takes another insane swing. But this time, miraculously, he makes solid contact. *Thwock!* The tiny white ball rockets in a majestic arc down the fairway. As it flies, it hooks left and sails into a line of trees on the fairway's left edge. After a few sharp cracks, there is silence.

"Wow," says Cat, watching in awe. "Nice hit. But I hope it isn't in the lagoon."

"What lagoon?"

"The Long Lagoon," says Cat. "It's a man-made lake that curves through four different holes."

"Why would men do that?" asks Cyril. "That's totally monkeys."

Cat shrugs.

"I mean, dude, come on," continues Cyril. "How can you achieve golfness if there's a bunch of water all over the place?"

"Cyril, water hazards are supposed to make shot selection more difficult," explains Cat.

"Why?"

"Because it's . . . more fun," says Cat.

"Why?"

"Let's go," sighs Cat.

The two pick up their bags and trudge, clubs clanking, down the fairway. As they approach the Scotch pines on the left side, a loud splashing noise arises from behind the tree line. At first it sounds like a big lawn sprinkler hissing to life. But then it transforms into a low, rumbling growl that slowly fades away.

"What the Barnaby was that?" asks Cyril.

Cat frowns. "Maybe they're dredging the lagoon for golf balls," she says.

"Cool!" says Cyril. "Let's check it out."

The two drop their golf bags in the rough along the trees and then start pushing through low pine branches. Just as they reach the moody, tree-darkened lagoon, a foamy jet of water, rising maybe twenty feet high, drops back onto the surface.

"What's up with the water?" asks Cyril.

"I don't know," Cat answers. "Some kind of fountain, I guess."

Cyril looks around. "So *this* . . . is the lost lagoon," he intones.

"The *Long* Lagoon," corrects Cat, looking around nervously. "Let's find your ball and get out of here."

Cyril gazes into the water. "I hope it's not in the drink," he says. "I didn't bring my, uh . . . scuba stuff."

Cyril hesitates on that last statement because he sees a vague shadow gliding underwater around a curve in the shoreline about thirty yards away. It disappears behind a grove of bald cypress trees jutting from the water.

Cyril frowns. "Gee, that's odd," he mumbles to himself.

Suddenly, an earsplitting shriek explodes from the grove. It is so loud that cypress leaves shudder.

Cyril and Cat freeze.

They hear something hiss and splash behind the cypress trees. Then Cat points out at the murky green water.

"Cyril," she whispers.

A dark shape, just under the surface, glides around the cypress grove.

It is very large.

As it moves, it pushes a ripple ahead . . . and leaves a bubble trail behind.

It heads directly toward Cat and Cyril.

③

SCARY MEN

As the huge underwater shadow approaches, Cyril notes its vaguely hand-shaped outline. Something about its color is very, very strange. The entity is a deep, oily black—so black, it seems to negate the water's surface glitter.

The Thing halts ten yards offshore, fluttering like fingers.

"What *is* it?" whispers Cat through clenched teeth.

"I don't know," whispers Cyril, grinning.

"What's it doing?"

"I don't know," Cyril says, still grinning.

Cat glances at Cyril. "Why are you grinning?"

Cyril grins at her. "I don't know," he whispers. "But it hurts."

Cat slaps him. The grin disappears.

"Thanks," says Cyril, rubbing his jaw.

More bubbles hiss to the surface above the huge, dark underwater-thing.

"Now what?" asks Cat, backing away from the water's edge.

"It's preparing to strike," squawks Cyril.

Say, maybe we should head back over to the Bixbys, like, right now.

Yeah, let's do that.

Jake Bixby exchanges a glance with Lucas as they listen to developments via their spy listeners. Then Jake looks up at the chain-link fence. It's a mere eight feet high, with no barbed wire on top.

Ha! Child's play for a Bixby.

"Let's go!" he says.

The brothers scramble over the fence, drop onto the soft golf course grass, and sprint like startled zebras . . . like zebras running on two hind legs, actually, going really fast, but with no stripes . . . like fast zebras, but without manes or fetlocks, but breathing hard like stampeding zebras . . . okay, forget the zebras, the two boys just run across the fairway.

They pass two golf bags lying on the ground and are just about to dive into the pine trees when Cat and Cyril burst out.

"Aaaaaaggghhh!" screams Cyril, colliding with Jake.

"Aaaaaaggghhh!" shouts Lucas, tripping over Jake and rolling into Cat's legs.

"Aaaaaaggghhh!" screams Cat as she does a full forward flip and lands directly atop Cyril.

"Aaaaaaggghhh!" screams Cyril again.

The fallen foursome scrambles to its eight or maybe nine or ten feet. It's hard to count feet accurately because everybody's all tangled up. Plus there are a few feet stuck in Cyril's hair. We can't see them. These feet may be lost forever.

"Holy carp swarm!" gasps Lucas.

"What's going on?" gasps Jake, trying to catch his breath after his wild zebralike sprint.[4]

"There's something weird in the lagoon," gasps Cat.

"Something *big*," gasps Cyril.

"Like what?" Lucas asks, excited. "An alligator?"

"Bigger," says Cyril.

"Does it have teeth?" shouts Lucas. He's really very excited right now.

"It was underwater," says Cyril. "We didn't see it clearly. But I'm pretty sure it was a plesiosaur with flippers." He bobs his eyebrows up and down. "If you know what I mean."

Jake gives him a skeptical look. "The Loch Ness monster is in our golf lagoon?"

Lucas gives his brother a wild-eyed stare. "Sure, why not? Let's go *look*!"

4. Hey, I like zebras.

"It's gone now," says Cyril.

Jake gives him a long stare. "Right," he says.

"Hey, Bixby," says Cat. "I saw it too."

Cyril seizes Jake by the shoulders. "Dude, I'm not kidding you," he says. "There's something huge swimming in the lagoon."

Cat nods in agreement. "It came right up to the shore for a second," she says.

"Like it was going to eat us," interjects Cyril.

"Then it sort of shimmered darkly and swam away," continues Cat. "Very odd."

Lucas looks disappointed. "It swam away?" he says.

"Yes."

"Swam away," repeats Jake, trying not to smirk. (Jake never actually smirks, but that doesn't mean he never has the *urge* to smirk.)

Cat crosses her arms and gives him a sharp look.

"Like I said, Bixby," she says with an edge. "It swam away."

Cyril waves his arms. "Into thin air," he says. "Or thin water, as it were." He lowers his voice and speaks quickly. "Of course the oxygen atom *is* a prominent part of the water molecule, so perhaps I'm correct on both counts."

Jake nods. "So the scary thing just left."

Cyril waggles his fingers. "Spooky, eh? One minute it's there, the next . . . it's gone." He makes his hands into claws. "*Arrrrrrrr!*"

"So, like, it didn't attack you or, or rise up and reveal its hideous nature or anything, like, monstrous or anything?" asks Lucas, still looking for some reason to get insanely excited.

"No."

Lucas frowns. "Then why were you guys running?" he asks.

Cyril claps him on the arm. "General unfocused fear," he says. He gazes up the fairway. "Plus we still have quite a bunch of golf to whack, apparently." He looks over at Cat. "Right?"

Cat gives Jake a tired look. "I'm teaching Cyril how to play golf," she explains. She gazes at Cyril. "It's been a tremendous mistake so far."

Cyril smiles with all of his teeth.

He says, "Guys, care to join us in some zany golf shenanigans?"

Lucas still can't get over this casual attitude toward possible monsters in the lagoon. "So what do you think it *was* . . . you know, this thing you saw?" He glances from Cat to Cyril.

"Just a shadow, I guess," says Cat.

Cyril gives her a look. "Yeah, but what about that shriek?"

"*Shriek?*" asks Lucas, his hope returning.

"Oh, that," says Cat. "Yeah."

"What shriek?" asks Lucas, bouncing on his toes. "What shriek?"

Cat looks at Lucas. "We heard a shriek," she says.

"Dudes, it came from behind the trees on the other side of the lagoon," says Cyril, pointing back toward the trees. "Some kind of *huuuuuge* animal. It sounded like a cross between an elephant and, and, like, a bobcat with a pizza." He suddenly grabs Jake by the shirt. "And I'm telling you, man, *it definitely had a Scottish accent.*"

Jake rolls his eyes. But then he grins.

"Awesome," he says.

Cat picks up her golf bag and slings it over her shoulder. "Actually, I think it was something mechanical," she says.

Cyril squints at her. "Mechanical?"

"Yeah," replies Cat. "It sounded harsh, almost metallic. Like a big drainage pump or something." She snaps her fingers. "And, hey, Cyril, I bet that's it. I bet that's what we saw in the water."

Cyril says, "You're saying that grisly hand-shaped hell-fiend was a pump?"

"Yes," says Cat. "Lots of lakes around here have those new Avalon submersible aerators. They're self-propelled so they move around, filtering out algae bloom and other vegetative occlusions."

The boys just stare at her.

Cat glances around at them. "What?" she says.

"That's just . . . incredibly impressive," says Lucas.

"Thank you," says Cat.

"But translate, please," says Jake.

"Okay," says Cat. She points toward the Long Lagoon. "Lots of gunk can build up in standing water like a lagoon," she says. "Especially algae. Stagnant water not only smells bad, it also lets insects like mosquitoes breed. So people put in fountains or underwater pump housings called aerators to filter the water and keep it moving."

"But . . . how do you know all that?" asks Lucas.

Cat grins. "My mom owns a landscaping service, and my dad works for Carrolton City Parks, which includes the reservoir." She glances over at the base of a nearby tree. "My knowledge of pond-related issues is madly intense and beastly . . . and, say, isn't that your golf ball there, Cyril?"

She points at a blotch of white in the high grass.

Cyril goes to it. "By Jove, it is." He smacks a fist into his palm. "Let's have a go at it, chaps!"

Jake watches with deep amusement as Cyril walks to his golf bag and then slides out a club.

"Cyril, that's your putter," says Cat.

"Excellent!" replies Cyril.

He steps to the ball and raises the putter straight up over his head. Then, with a horrific karate shriek, he chops the club straight downward onto the ball.

"*Fore!*" he shouts.

As the gruesome attack continues, the author quickly fades this scene to black.

• • •

Later that evening, a small girl with dark eyes and long black hair in a high ponytail walks down a sidewalk in downtown Carrolton.

This "girl" is no ordinary girl, of course. This, my friends, is Lexi Lopez.

She's a spy.

Lexi wears ear buds connected to an iPod on her belt. The music must be pretty tight because every few seconds she does a slick crossover dance step. When she reaches Ye Olde Ice-Cream Shoppe, she spins in a graceful pirouette and enters.

As she enters the shop, Lexi sees a large young man in a white apron peering out a side window into the alley. The shaggy, unshaven fellow also wears a white, wedge-shaped clerk's cap. He leans his considerable weight on a wet mop clasped in his hands.

Lexi's eyes brighten. "Hey, dude!" she shouts out.

The young man jumps. Then, irritated, he glances over his shoulder at Lexi.

He says, "Lopez."

"You've been gone for, like, two months," says Lexi, plucking off her ear buds.

"Yes," he says. "Two months. And it was so peaceful without loud children around." He turns to face Lexi. The shop's logo is on the front of his apron, plus a tag that reads, I'M MARCO AND I LOVE ICE CREAM!

"So what are you doing *here*?" she asks.

"I'm not sure yet," says the huge young man.

Lexi points at him. "Why are you wearing that apron?"

He looks down at it. Then he looks at her and says, "I'm Marco . . . and I love ice cream."

"You *work* here?" Lexi's jaw drops and clatters to the floor. She picks it up, reattaches it to the bottom of her face, and says, "Why?"

"Like I said, I'm not sure yet," says Marco. He moves away from the window and starts mopping the floor. As he swabs the mop behind the counter, he says, "They didn't tell me why."

"They?" says Lexi.

Marco stops mopping. "Do you want to buy some ice cream? If not, get out before I call the cops."

Lexi grins. "I want a cone."

Marco glances at the window again. Suddenly, he drops his mop, hops over the counter, and hurries to the pane. He presses his face against the glass.

"Did you see that?" he asks.

Lexi frowns. "No."

Marco tries to look down the alley toward the back of the store.

Lexi says, "Hey, I want a cone."

"Help yourself," says Marco, waving a hand toward the glass cases filled with big tubs of colorful ice cream and sherbets.

"Really?"

"Yes, and be quiet, will you?"

Lexi steps behind the counter. She grabs a metal scoop from a small hot-water sink and jabs it eagerly into a tub of caramel-fudge swirl. Grunting with effort, she curls up a big frosty ball. Then she smashes the gooey goodness into a waffle cone.

She glances up at Marco, who still peers up the alley. With a small grin, she scoops up a second ice-cream ball and mashes it atop the first. As she does this, she notices a sheet of paper entitled "Employment Application" near the cash register. The name of the applicant is "Rossi, Marco."

"Marco Rossi?" says Lexi. "That sounds Italian."

"It is."

"You're Italian?"

"My dad was," says Marco.

"He *was*?" says Lexi. "What is he now?"

"Dead."

"Oh," says Lexi. Her shoulders slump. "I'm sorry."

Marco puts his hands on his hips, still looking out the window. He doesn't speak.

"Marco," calls Lexi, "who are *they*?"

Without looking, Marco says, "Men."

"What men?"

Marco, exasperated, turns to her again. "Don't you ever just . . . go home and read?"

Lexi ducks under the end of the counter and approaches him. "I read a lot," she says.

Marco looks at her. "Go read," he says.

"So, what men?"

"Read!"

"I just want to know what men."

Marco suddenly jerks his head up, looking past Lexi toward the shop entrance. "Crap!" he exclaims.

Lexi spins around to see a long black sedan pulling up to the curb just outside the shop front. Marco quickly grabs Lexi by the shoulders and steers her toward the back of the store.

"Out the back door," he says with urgency.

"Are those the men?" asks Lexi.

Marco guides her through a storage room, opens a metal door, and scoots her out. "There's a four-foot, chain-link fence at the head of the alley," he says, pointing. "Will that be a problem for you?"

She spins and glares up at him. But then she sees the dark glitter in his eyes. "You're kidding," she says.

"Right," he says. "Get out of here."

Marco turns and hurries back into the shop.

Lexi watches him for a second, and then scoots down the back alley to the corner of the building. She stops and looks wistfully down at her huge double-dip cone. If anybody can scale a four-foot fence while holding ice cream, it's Lexi Lopez. But Marco's urgency has her a bit spooked.

Sadly, she tosses the cone into a Dumpster parked

against the shop's back wall. Then she rounds the corner to the chain-link fence. Just as she grabs it, ready to climb, she freezes.

Ahead, the alley runs along the shop's side to the street. There, the hood of the black sedan extends halfway across the alley opening. Two men in black suits and sunglasses lean against the front of the car, gazing down the street ahead of them.

"Sentries!" gasps Lexi.

One of them glances up the alley. Seeing Lexi, he jerks to attention and says something to his partner, who turns to look too.

Lexi ducks quickly back behind the corner by the Dumpster. Then she scans the area.

A tall wooden fence, maybe ten or twelve feet high, runs along the back alley on the side opposite the ice-cream shop; a four-story office building rises directly behind it. Lexi spots a shipping pallet leaning at an angle against the fence. Its wood slats run horizontally.

Just around the corner, she hears a man's deep voice quietly say, "Roger that, we're tracking movement in the back alley, over."

In a flash, Lexi scampers across the alley and up the shipping pallet, then grabs the top of the fence and swings over. She hangs on the other side for a second, checking below. Then she drops lightly to the ground.

Just as she lands, she hears a humming noise behind her. She turns to look.

A large metal garage door slowly slides upward.

The door is on a delivery dock at the back of the office building. As the door rises, Lexi can see the feet of several men behind it. Their boots and pants are white.

She darts behind a stack of white boxes labeled AMBS. This is some sort of delivery yard, with shipments stacked everywhere. She carefully peeks around the white boxes.

Three men step through the garage door onto the delivery dock.

Lexi frowns.

Beekeepers? she thinks.

THE CREEPY CRATE

Lucas Bixby jogs along Willow Road, heading toward the Carrolton Business District. He was supposed to meet his best buddy Lexi Lopez for ice cream twenty minutes ago, but something important delayed him. He adjusts the mouthpiece of the Spy Link headset hooked over his ear.

"Lima Lima, do you read me?" he says. "Hey, Lima Lima, are you out there? This is Lima Bravo, over."

Beep!

Hear that beep? The one coming from the backpack slung on Lucas's back?

That's what delayed him.

Beep!

That beep you hear comes from a device known as the Omega Link. All Team Spy Gear fans know about the Omega Link. It's the mysterious "com-link" (communications link) that receives mysterious message-clues from mysterious sources.

Beep!

Whenever the Omega Link receives a message, the device beeps to announce the arrival. Right now, for example, the *beeping* has Lucas in a frenzy of excitement because this, incredibly, amazingly, is the *second* Omega message of the day. After months of silence!

Lucas wrestles the backpack off his back, stabs his hand into its guts, and rips out its silver heart:[5] the slim titanium casing with no knobs, no controls, nothing but a display screen. He holds it up to his eyes. After staring at the new message for a moment, Lucas nods.

"And *that* confirms my hypothesis," he says to himself, nodding grimly.

A voice speaks in his ear. **And what hypothesis would that be, Heisenberg?** says the voice. Hey, it's Cyril's voice.

"Cyril? Is that you?" asks Lucas.

Yes, it's me.

"What are you doing on the Spy Link channel?" asks Lucas.

Trying to reach your brother, says Cyril. **I just finished the golf tomfoolery with Cat and now I'm free for some loitering, which to me is what Sunday is supposed to be all about.**

"Cyril, I got another Omega message," says Lucas.

5. Gross!

What? Another one?

"Yes, another one."

Is it as stupid as the first one?

"Stupider."

Insanity! says Cyril. What's it say?

Lucas stares at the Omega Link display. "Wimps," he says.

What?

"W-I-M-P-S," spells Lucas. "Wimps."

Wimps?

"Wimps."

Silence on Cyril's end. Then: It's talking smack to us?

"Apparently."

Especially after the first message today, says Cyril.

Just three hours ago, not long after the golf course incident, the Bixby boys were shoveling out their bedroom when the Omega Link first beeped.[6] After a brotherly "contest" (i.e., brawl) over who would be the first to see the transmission, the two Bixbys decided to view it simultaneously. Thus both Jake and Lucas were mystified at the very same moment by the first message of the day:

M A C H O

"First MACHO, then WIMPS," says Lucas, shaking his head. "What's going on here?"

6. Like all brothers who share a bedroom, Jake and Lucas Bixby accumulate stuff that forms sedimentary layers. This must be excavated every few months. During one such dig, Jake uncovered the skeleton of a Mexican Rhombus. Another time, Lucas found a side entrance to Hell.

Apparently, the device is challenging our manhood, says Cyril.

"Yeah, well, when Lexi finds out about this, she'll kick its butt," says Lucas with a thin smile. "Speaking of which, I can't get her to answer. The girl always forgets to wear her Spy Link headset."

Inexcusable! bellows Cyril.

Breaking, breaking, ten-forty-forms, hisses Lexi's voice in a sudden, urgent whisper over the channel. *Can anybody hear me? Guys? Over?*

"Whoa, speak of the devil," says Lucas, grinning. "There you are, over."

Lucas? Is that you?

"Roger, this is Lima Bravo acknowledging," answers Lucas. "Why are you whispering, over?"

Dude, I'm hiding, replies Lexi. She sounds very tense. Then she adds: *I think I need backup, like, right now.*

Look, Lucas and Lexi have been best friends for something like eighty years, ever since meeting on the monkey bars at Loch Ness Elementary School, way back in kindergarten. Lucas knows Lexi better than he knows anybody except for his own brother. And in all those eighty or ninety years, he has never, ever heard Lexi say something like "I think I need backup, like, right now." Not in that tone of voice.

Lucas bursts into a wild sprint. "I'll be there in ninety!"

he exclaims, voice shaking from the sprint. "Where are you, over?"

Behind the ice-cream shop, whispers Lexi.

"Are you in trouble?" gasps Lucas.

Sort of, says Lexi quietly. Then: Can't talk now. Stay on the line.

"Roger that, roger that!" says Lucas.

Cyril cuts in. I'm heading to your house now, he says. I'll get Jake, and we'll be there in ten.

Suddenly, Jake's voice cuts in. Hey, I'm on, I copy everything. Lexi, Lucas, I'm on the way. Cyril, head straight downtown, pronto.

Gotcha, says Cyril. I'm stumbling insanely in that direction, even as we speak.

Keep talking to that girl, bro, adds Jake.

"Roger that," gasps Lucas, now breaking the world record for the Willow Road Dash. Hey, if there's one thing Lucas can do really, really well, it's "keep talking." "Lexi dog, give me something so I know you're alive. Just a 'pssst.'"

Pssst!

"Good! Keep it up!"

Pssst!

Lexi watches three men in bulky white coveralls that drape them from neck to hand to foot.

She's right: They look like beekeepers.

Each one also wears white gloves, white boots, and a hard hat hung with netting that covers the face and then tucks into a thick-looking vest. The men stand on the loading dock doing . . . nothing.

Hmmm.

They stand and stare straight ahead . . . although it's tough to tell exactly what they're looking at from behind the netting.

This is very strange, thinks Lexi.

The dock is a good forty feet or so from where she hides. But the complete silence and lack of movement makes her afraid to even whisper. So she continues the quiet *pssst* sounds into the Spy Link mouthpiece, and pulls back behind the white boxes to survey the situation.

Above her, the boxes are stacked high, nearly the height of the fence behind her.

Lexi sees several good footholds where boxes overlap crookedly.

She smiles.

She's about to give another *pssst* signal to the boys when she hears the loud rumble of an approaching vehicle. She peeks around the boxes again. The roar gets louder. Yes, a truck is approaching; its front grille creeps into view on one side of the office building. It looks like the silver snout of a huge beast.

The three men on the dock continue staring straight

ahead. Then, in perfect unison, their heads turn to face the truck.

A snaky chill slithers up Lexi's spine.

"Okay," she murmurs. "*That's* creepy."

"What's creepy?" replies Lucas, running up Main Street, approaching Ye Olde Ice-Cream Shoppe from the south. "What's creepy, Lima Lima? Over."

These guys, says Lexi. Something is not natural about them.

Up ahead, Lucas sees his brother, Jake, sprinting across the intersection from the west. "Yo, bro. I got you marked," he calls.

Jake skids to a halt and waits as Lucas jogs up to him.

"Lexi, we're right in front of the ice-cream shop," says Jake into his Spy Link mouthpiece. "Are you still okay?" The Bixbys can hear the loud gunning of a truck engine somewhere behind the shop.

I'm cool, says Lexi. Is the black car still there?

The boys look around. The street is deserted.

"No," says Lucas.

Then get Marco, says Lexi. He's inside. I have news for him.

"Wait," says Lucas. "You're saying *Marco* is inside the ice-cream shop?"

Yeah, says Lexi. He works there. But he doesn't know why yet.

Jake and Lucas look at each other.

"Okay," says Jake.

The brothers hustle into the shop. It is deserted.

"Nobody's here, Lexi," says Jake. "The shop is empty."

Try the back room, she suggests.

Jake leads the way behind the counter into the storage area and office. It, too, is deserted.

"There's nobody here, kid," says Jake.

Maybe he left with the men in the black car, says Lexi.

"Where are you?" asks Lucas.

Lexi directs the Bixbys outside. As the boys step through the back door into the alley behind the shop, the roar of the truck is louder. They also hear the distinctive *beep! beep! beep!* warning of a commercial vehicle backing up. Lexi describes her location and the layout on her side of the fence.

Hey, they're unloading something from the truck, says Lexi.

"You sure you're okay, Lima Lima?" asks Lucas.

Oh yeah, she says happily. **Hey, the driver just got out of the truck and went inside. Now's your chance.** She actually chortles. **Come on, guys! Come spy with me!**

Both Jake and Lucas scramble up the slats of the same shipping pallet that Lexi climbed earlier. Jake pulls himself up the fence and peeks over. A big white delivery truck is backed up to the building.

Lucas climbs up next to Jake. He looks down and sees

Lexi waving at them from behind her stack of boxes.

"Let's go," says Jake.

The Bixbys hang from the top railing and quickly drop to the ground. As they scurry behind the white boxes, Lexi and Lucas high-five.

Jake says, "Cyril? We're with Lexi. Dude, where are you?"

Cyril's voice, gasping horribly, echoes in their ears. This is Gaucho Excelsior reporting, he says. All units, be advised [gasp] I'm going into Code Orange surveillance mode. [gasp] Repeat, that's Code Orange. [gasp] All systems are go for Code Orange [gasp gasp] maneuver.

"What's Code Orange?" asks Lexi.

"I believe it's a state of total physical collapse," says Jake.

Roger that, Jake, says Cyril. We have external limbs shutting down in five, four, three . . .

Jake grins. "Dude, are you nearby?"

Uh, I'm now at the front door of the ice-cream shop, answers Cyril.

"Okay, just stay put," says Jake. "Keep an eye on the street out front."

There is a pause. Then, in a deep voice, Cyril says, Roger that, Houston.

"Okay, good," says Jake.

I'm watching it very closely, Jake.

"Good," says Jake.

I think it's moving.

"The street?"

Yes.

"Okay," says Jake, amused.

I believe it's heading north, says Cyril.

"Okay, keep it marked."

Will do.

"If you get to Minneapolis, give us a call," says Jake.

Roger that, Delta Leader. Over and out.

Now the Bixbys and Lexi peek around the white boxes. Across the loading yard, the rumbling delivery truck still blocks the view of the dock. Their view of the truck is head on, but they can hear loud scraping noises, as if something heavy is being dragged.

Lexi frowns. "Why are the bee guys so quiet?" she whispers.

Lucas looks at her. "What do you mean?"

"Nobody's talking," says Lexi. She looks puzzled. "I'm telling you, these guys are weird."

Suddenly a man in a gray jumpsuit with a low-slung cap and sunglasses walks around the truck.

"That's the driver!" whispers Lexi.

The kids pull their heads back behind the boxes. Lucas digs into his gadget backpack and pulls out three Micro Periscopes. The team uses these gadgets to spy unseen around the boxes again.

The truck engine fires up.

Then the vehicle drives off around the building. As it leaves, Jake notes the corporate logo and name, AMBS, emblazoned on its side. Up on the dock, the three men in white garb all stand around a long, metallic-looking crate about the size of a coffin.

"Beekeepers?" says Lucas.

"Exactly," says Lexi.

The men stare down at the odd container as if unsure what to do next. Perhaps understandably so: An odd humming sound rises from the crate. Then something else odd happens. All three men start shrugging their shoulders, up and down.

"What the donkey are they *doing*?" wonders Jake.

"What *is* it?" asks Lucas, a little excited, staring at the coffin-size crate.

"What's that *weird* sound?" asks Lexi.

Hey, those are good questions. Here's another: *What's the square root of Bob Stevens?* I've never seen a satisfactory answer to that one, and neither has Bob.[7] But good spies are always looking for answers to the hard questions. At this very moment, for example, Lucas pulls another gadget out of his backpack.

The gadget—a Spy Supersonic Ear—is a listening dish that captures sound from the direction you point it, then amplifies (makes louder) the sound and funnels it into a set of headphones worn on the left knee. Lucas

7. Bob lives somewhere, but I'm not sure.

Bixby slides the headphones over his left knee and holds up the listening dish. Then he stops to think for a second, puts down the dish, and slides the headphones over his ears instead.[8]

Lucas peeks around the boxes again.

The three beekeeper-men stand around the crate, still shrugging.

Lucas points the listening dish at the crate. His eyes grow big.

"What is it?" asks Jake. "What do you hear?"

Lucas rips the headphones off his knee, I mean ears, and gives them to Jake. The older Bixby slips them over his . . . uh . . . ears and listens.

Many little things scratch and clatter around inside the crate. The clattering is harsh: Metal on metal, it sounds like. A faint buzzing or hissing adds a constant hum to the background.

Jake pulls off the headphones.

"Whoa!" he whispers. "That gives me the creeps."

"Those freaking *beekeepers* give me the creeps," says Lexi.

Then, as Jake hands the headphones to Lexi for a listen, several loud screeches suddenly arise from the crate. The three kids freeze in fright. The scrabble inside the crate intensifies too.

In their Spy Link earpieces, the Bixbys and Lexi hear Cyril gasp.

8. The real clue here is that they're called "headphones" and not "kneephones." Ha! I'm really disappointed none of you figured this out and called me so I could change it.

"Cyril?" calls Jake. "Do you hear that?"

Yes! says Cyril.

"You can hear it out on the *street*?" whispers Jake.

I'm in the alley now, says Cyril. **And guys . . . I know that sound.**

"From where?"

The lagoon! says Cyril.

Lucas almost swoons with excitement. "You mean the monster thing you heard with Cat?" He quickly jams the Spy Supersonic Ear into his pack.

Exactly! says Cyril. **Except this one's, like . . . smaller.**

Another rasping screech rises from the crate. This one is piercing, louder and deeper than the last. The metallic clattering and banging gets stronger. It sounds different now too: less frenzied, but more powerful.

On the dock, the three men in white back away from the rocking, rattling crate.

They disappear into the building.

5

THE BLACK HAND

Without thinking, Jake puts a hand on the shoulders of the two smaller kids.

His jaw is tense.

"Let's get out of here," he says calmly.

Up on the dock, the coffinlike crate is now shaking so hard, it moves a few inches. Lexi stares at it. "I'm scared," she says. But, as if mesmerized, she takes a step toward it.

"Yeah, me too," says Jake, pulling her back. "Let's go."

He pulls a box off the top of the stack. It weighs less than he expects; it's empty. He sets it on the ground and quickly grabs another. Lucas sees the plan and grabs a box too, stacking it on Jake's. Soon they have a small pyramid of boxes.

"Quickly!" says Jake. "Lexi, go!"

Lexi scrambles up the three-high box-stack and, with

a nimble leap, grabs the top of the fence. Lucas scales the boxes beneath her and gives Lexi a boost; she goes up and over. Now Lucas jumps and grabs the fence top.

On the dock, an emergency siren starts blaring.

"Crud!" says Lucas.

"Hurry, dude!" says Jake, climbing the boxes. He boosts Lucas, who slips over the fence.

Finally Jake follows.

He has to dig his toes hard into the fence to scoot upward—after all, there's nobody to boost *him* up—but, kids, here's where soccer muscles *really* come in handy.[9] Jake also gets an extra boost of adrenaline when The Shrieking Crate Thing rattles so hard, its cage falls off the loading dock with a loud clatter. Plus there's the angry yelling men who burst through the loading door, and so forth. Plus the small explosion.

Jake practically flies over the fence top.

When he lands in the alley, he sees the rest of Team Spy Gear, including Cyril, crouched and waiting for him.

"Holy wowsa!" he says.

"What was that explosion?" asks Lucas, wide-eyed.

"I have no idea," says Jake. "I didn't look back. Come on!"

He leads the team over the chain-link fence and down the side alley to the front of Ye Olde Ice-Cream Shoppe.

9. Jake started soccer at age two, shortly after his mother, Mrs. Bixby, read an article entitled "Are Other Kids *Better* Than Your Kids? Here's How to Find Out!" The article linked early soccer skills to overall child betterness.

When they round the corner, they find Marco standing in the front doorway.

"Marco!" exclaims Jake.

"Bixby," replies Marco. He nods.

"Something very strange is going on back there," says Lucas, pointing down the alley.

"I heard," says Marco. He looks down at Lexi. "What's up, Lopez?" he asks. "You look excited."

"I'm scared," she says.

"But you're smiling," says Marco.

Lexi smiles bigger. "I *like* being scared," she says.

Marco nods. "Come on in," he says, gesturing into the shop. "Let's talk."

Dr. Tim's pickup truck pulls into the driveway of a white, split-level home on the west side of Ridgeview Drive, just north of Platte Park.

A short, stout, balding man hurries down from the front porch, waving.

Dr. Tim steps out of his truck and nods. "Hello, Jack."

"This way, Dr. Tim," says the short man.

The man, Jack Barge, leads Dr. Tim around the house. His property backs up to the Carrolton Reservoir. It's a very nice property. A small boat dock extends from the backyard into the water.

Mr. Barge makes quick, short strides to a small flower garden near the waterfront.

"This is where I found it," he says, pointing at a big hole in the ground about two feet wide and equally deep.

Dr. Tim crouches to look. "And you say you tried to *flood* them out?" he asks.

"I did." Mr. Barge nods.

"And it didn't work," says Dr. Tim.

"Correct," says Mr. Barge. "So I just dug it up."

Dr. Tim nods. "The entire colony?"

"Correct."

Dr. Tim squints menacingly at the man. "You didn't just *poison* them, did you, Jack?"

"Of course not, Dr. Tim," says Mr. Barge, suddenly sweating and pulling at his collar. Then he rubs the top of his head: *Skreek! Skreek! Skreek!* He adds, "I know better than that."

"Good." Dr. Tim picks up a small garden spade sitting near the hole and pokes at the disturbed dirt. "What did you do with it?"

"I dumped it in the reservoir," says Mr. Barge.

"Okay," says Dr. Tim. "So . . . what exactly happened when you tried to drown the critters?"

Mr. Barge squints, remembering. "Well, I ran my garden hose down here and jammed it right into the anthill, or whatever it is," he says, stroking his chin. "Then I turned it on full blast. Water flushed the bugs right up. Worked very well. Or so I thought."

"And then?" asks Dr. Tim.

"And then I noticed this." Mr. Barge walks over to a small storage shed, opens the door, and pulls out a large glass jar. He brings it back and hands it to Dr. Tim, who holds it up.

The jar is full of water.

Inside, swarms of eight-legged insects swim around gracefully underwater.

Back at Ye Olde Ice-Cream Shoppe, Team Spy Gear finishes its report to Marco as he shovels scoops of ice cream into cones for the kids. Then Marco pulls a slender, gleaming MacBook out of a leather carrying case stashed behind the counter. He sits at a table, opens the laptop, and starts typing.

"What are you doing?" asks Jake.

"Making a report," says Marco.

"To who?" asks Jake.

Marco just types. After a few seconds he glances up to see Jake staring at him. "I can't really say, Bixby," he says finally.

"To the Agency, right?" says Jake.

"I can't say."

"Give me a break," says Jake. He looks down at his ice-cream cone.

Marco's eyes darken. "Look," he says. "It's not that I don't trust children. Frankly, you've done far more for the Agency than they've done for you."

Jake looks up. "You're protecting us," he says.

Marco sighs and meets Jake's gaze.

"Here's the deal," he says. "The Agency put you in physical danger recently. I'm not too happy about that. And there's something new going on now . . . in theory . . . that I don't want you kids anywhere *near*."

"You're protecting us," repeats Jake grimly.

"Exactly."

Lexi steps forward. "Maybe we don't *want* protection."

Marco looks at her. "Was I *talking* to the little girl?"

Lexi slugs his arm, hard.

Marco winces. "That . . . actually hurt," he says.

Lexi raises her fist. "Say hello to Buster," she says.

Now Marco manages a half-smile. He starts typing again. He says, "Go home." He reads something on the screen and adds, "Sorry, Bixby."

Jake gives Lucas a quick look and says, "Okay, thanks." He starts heading for the door.

Lucas and the others just stare at him.

Jake glances back at them. "Come on, guys," he says. "Let's go home."

"And do what?" says Cyril testily. "Play with dolls?"

"We could do that," says Jake. "Or we could try to decode those new Omega Link messages."

Marco stops typing. He says, "What?"

Now Cyril grins like a shark. "Oh, yeah," he says. "Those."

"Yes, Cyril," says Jake. "The *first* one, and then . . . you know . . . the *second* one."

Now Marco looks at Lucas. "Something came through the Omega Link?" he asks.

"No," replies Lucas. Then, after a second, he says, "Wait. I mean, yes. Yes on that, actually." He smiles sweetly.

Marco stands up. "Okay, okay."

Jake gazes innocently at him. "Okay *what*?" he asks.

Marco reaches down and closes his laptop. Then he looks around at the foursome.

He says, "So . . . let's talk some more."

Just then, a group of high school kids bursts into the ice-cream shop, all jabbering excitedly. They wear T-shirts over swimsuits.

"Dude, Jeremy and Amber saw it too!" says one boy. "*Everyone* at the res saw it!" (Most kids call Carrolton Reservoir "the res.")

"It went right under our sailboat!" says a girl.

"Yeah, all those Santana middies on the beach saw it too," says a duck.

"Middies" is a local Carrolton slang term. Kids refer to the students at Carlos Santana Middle School as "middies."

Jake steps up to the older kids. "Excuse me," he says. "What are you guys talking about?"

One of the girls looks at him like he's an idiot or a

little kid. "Like, the monster?" she says. "Duh? Like, in the reservoir?" She rolls her eyes at one of the older boys and says, "*Whatever!*"

Jake persists. "You saw something in the reservoir?"

The girl sighs and pulls out her cell phone. "Check it out, fanboy." She pushes a few buttons on the phone: *Beep! Beep!* "I got a totally good shot of it on my cell phone camera." She holds it out to Jake.

The other Team Spy Gear members crowd in beside Jake and gaze at the phone's small display screen.

The bottom third of the digital shot shows a boat's gunwale. The top two thirds show the bright green surface of the reservoir. The water glitters in the sun. Just beneath the surface is a shadow.

"Oh, my, God," says Cyril.

It's shaped like a huge dark hand.

Monday morning, 8:11 a.m. The next day.

Tales of the "reservoir monster" spread like a foot fungus through the halls of Carlos Santana Middle School. If you've ever had foot fungus, you know what I'm talking about. If you've *never* had foot fungus, then you *don't* know what I'm talking about, but then your feet don't smell like putrefying fish guts, so actually you come out ahead on this one.

Anyway, right now, four minutes before the first-period bell, the buzz has grown to the point of mass lunacy.

Jake and Cyril lean against lockers, observing the madness.

"Some of these people scare me," says Cyril.

Jake nods. A howling pack of seventh graders runs past with a roast boar on a spit. Jake watches them and says, "Fear makes kids do weird things."

"Yes," agrees Cyril. "It rips apart the social fabric. Discipline breaks down." He gestures toward several girls screaming and bashing out windows in the front lobby with live ferrets. "Kids lose all sense of perspective when the possibility of a monster arises."

Suddenly Jake's cell phone rings.

He usually turns off his phone inside the building, to comply with school rules. But today he left the phone on for a reason. Flipping it open, Jake checks the incoming number.

"Yep," he says. "It's Marco. Finally." He answers quickly. "What-up, old man?"

"It wasn't them," says Marco.

Jake nearly drops his phone. "What?"

"It wasn't them."

Jake gives Cyril a big look. "The Omega messages weren't from the Agency?"

"Nope," answers Marco.

Jake glances at his XP-6 Spy Watch. "Dude, our math class starts in, like, three minutes," he says. "Quickly, what else do you know about it?"

"Me?" says Marco. "Nothing."

"Well then, what does the Agency know about 'macho wimps'?"

"Nothing," says Marco.

"They know nothing," repeats Jake to Cyril.

Cyril starts applauding.

"And so . . . what now?" asks Jake.

"They're working on it," says Marco.

Jake turns to Cyril. "They're working on it," he repeats.

"Ah, good," says Cyril. "Top men, no doubt. I guess we can rest easy now." He reaches out and grabs a passing sixth grader. "Jeeves, bring me another brandy, please," he says.

The sixth grader screams. Cyril lets him go.

Jake snickers. "So that's it?" he says to Marco. "That's all we get from the Agency?"

"For now," answers Marco.

"I mean, like, do they think it's a joke?" continues Jake. "Who's sending us these wimp and macho messages if they aren't?"

"Maybe a hacker," says Marco.

"Or maybe Viper," says Jake. "Maybe he's taunting us."

"Maybe," says Marco. "But I really doubt he can hack into the channel this time." Marco pauses. "Unless he's got moles planted inside the Agency. He pauses again. I can't say that would surprise me, given some of the clowns I've met there."

Jake hesitates for a second. Then, looking at Cyril again, he says, "Okay, Marco, so we kept our end of the bargain. We gave you the Omega transmissions. Now it's your turn."

"I'll meet you after school," says Marco. At Stoneship.

"And you'll tell us everything you know," insists Jake.

"Yes," says Marco. "But they're keeping a lot of new stuff on a need-to-know basis . . . and, dude, I'm not on the A-list yet."

"But any day now," says Jake, grinning.

"Later, Bixby," says Marco, and clicks off.

Jake turns off his cell phone just as the first bell rings.

"Jake, our education beckons us," says Cyril. He straightens his hair and clutches his backpack. "Ready, old chap?"

"Ready," says Jake.

With a howl, the boys dive into the writhing mass of students that flows like lava down the hall.

Three hours later, Lucas Bixby sits at a workstation in a back alcove of the school's Computer Lab. He often spends his lunch period here, eating as he researches favorite inventions and technologies.

Today, however, Lucas has other plans.

First, he slips on a pair of Spy Vision Specs. These are tinted glasses with a small mirror attachment that lets the wearer see what's behind him. Lucas doesn't want anyone sneaking up unannounced for the next fifteen minutes.

Next, he pulls a small, cylinder-shaped gadget out of his backpack—a Spy Voice Trap. He holds it to his mouth, pushes its record button, and says quietly, "Heads up, Lucas." Then he places the gadget on a nearby desk so its light-sensitive motion detector points across the room. This gives Lucas an added level of security against unauthorized approach.

Finally, Lucas pulls his Spy Gear Casebook from the backpack. He flips it open and takes a quick peek at the two most recent entries.

"Macho, wimps," he reads. "Weird."

Then he grabs the mouse and clicks open the school search engine. He starts typing on the workstation keyboard.

First, he types "MACHO."

A preliminary search brings up several results. The first few refer to the common Spanish word, which means "male" or "manly." Lucas also finds several references to MACHO as an acronym used by astronomers. It stands for Massive Compact Halo Object and refers to any large, heavy object in space such as a black hole or a burned-out dark star—distant objects with a lot of mass but so dark, they're almost undetectable.

"Surely that's not what the Omega message is talking about," mumbles Lucas as he skims the entry.

Next, he types "WIMP" into the search engine. This

time he gets entries referring to the common slang meaning of "a weak, cowardly, or ineffective person." A second meaning is a computer-world acronym for the usual way people interact with a computer: This WIMP stands for Window, Icon, Menu, Pointing device.

"No way," murmurs Lucas.

Then he finds another meaning. "WIMP" is also an acronym for a term used in particle physics: Weakly Interactive Massive Particles. Lucas reads that these particles are hypothetical—that is, they have not been actually discovered yet. But physicists believe that some type of particle, much smaller than a normal atom, is the basic bit of matter in the universe. We can't see or detect a WIMP because it's so small and passes right through regular matter like you or me.

"Interesting," says Lucas.

Behind him he hears, "Heads up, Lucas," from the Spy Voice Trap. He glances up into the rearview mirror on his Spy Vision Specs . . . and sees Lexi Lopez crossing the computer lab toward him.

Lucas spins his chair around to face her. "Dude," he says as she approaches.

"Dude," she replies. They lock fingers, snap them, and then point at each other. "Got anything?"

"Not really," says Lucas. "But did you know that something like ninety percent of the matter in the universe is invisible?"

"You mean, like, ghosts and stuff?" says Lexi.

"Not exactly," says Lucas. He spins his chair back around and looks at the "WIMP" info on the monitor. "It says right here, scientists observing the motion of galaxies have figured out that there's a gazillion tons of dark stuff out there that we just can't see." He points at the screen. "They call it 'dark matter.'"

"Sounds spooky," says Lexi.

"Yeah," agrees Lucas.

"Heads up, Lucas," says the Spy Voice Trap.

Lucas spins his chair around again . . . just in time to see the approach of a predatory pack of hissing, hungry-looking girls. His face goes white.

"We're dead meat," he whispers.

Lexi also turns to look and gasps.

"*The Flesh Eaters!*" she exclaims in horror.

Jake and Cyril both sit slumped in their Language Arts class, staring at a tall, skinny kid named Aaron Urlchucker. Aaron stands in front of the class, sweating like a pig. Wait, no. Pigs don't sweat, actually.[10] Actually, Aaron is sweating like a zebra giving a speech to a bunch of lions.

From the back of the room, the teacher, Mrs. Porkbat, calls out, "Please proceed, Aaron."

"I can't," says Aaron.

10. Did you know that? I certainly didn't. But my editor did. She's an expert at making things sweat, and made me change it.

"But you must," says Mrs. Porkbat.

"But I can't," says Aaron.

Today is Poetry Day. Each student in Mrs. Porkbat's class must read aloud a poem he or she has written. Some kids enjoy the experience. Others find it terrifying. Jake hates it, but he's already finished his reading, so right now he slumps in a pleasant state that's halfway between waking and coma.

Cyril, on the other hand, has been looking forward to this day for weeks. He's worked hard on his master poem, "Confessions of a Large Cheese." But he slumps because he probably won't get to read it until tomorrow. The period's almost over. After Aaron finishes and his striped carcass is torn into large chunks, there's time for only one more reader.

"Today's last poet will be Barbie Bickle," says Mrs. Porkbat.

The class moans.

Jake sits up and watches as Barbie walks slowly to the front of the classroom. Today her clothes are purple; so is her hair. Some days she's blue. Other days green. Most kids make fun of Barbie because she's so different. But Jake has always found her odd looks and manner interesting and even, well, kind of cool.

Barbie turns to face the class. She unfolds a sheet of paper.

"'The Black Hand,'" she announces.

Then she reads a chilling poem. Its central image is a huge black hand that arises, dripping, from a dark lake one night. It slaps down onto the dark shore and dissolves into the reeds and grasses with a harrowing hiss.

Jake looks over at Cyril, who sits as if paralyzed, with his mouth wide open.

"Wow," he whispers.

"'Where does it go?'" reads Barbie. And then she lowers the paper and recites the final lines from memory, looking around the room:

**"'A shriek divides into ten shrieks, into a hundred,
A thousand, a million.
Amphibious fear slithers ashore, its trillion legs crawling,
Now divided by eight.
Then recombines the bit-matter into The Black Hand,
The Shrieking Shadow.'"**

The classroom is dead silent as Barbie finishes. Then she slowly walks back to her desk.

6

DARK, DARK MATTERS

Kids, if you've already read Books 1, 2, 3, and 4 of the Spy Gear Adventure series, you probably remember Stoneship Woods. It's that carnivorous forest right in the center of Carrolton. In the spring, Stoneship Woods is very beautiful, but also very hungry. After the long, cold winter, the trees really need the kind of protein boost that only human flesh can provide. Many meat-loving fauna and insect species make their home here, as well. So if you walk into Stoneship Woods in April or May, consider yourself a food item on the local menu.

Unfortunately, Team Spy Gear headquarters is right in the middle of these woods.

"That cottonwood is following us," says Cyril, walking backward and gazing up at a large tree.

Ahead of him, both Bixby boys and Lexi push through

a stand of young pines. "Dude, I used to think you were just paranoid," says Jake. "But I don't remember these pines being here yesterday." A pine branch reaches out and slaps his face. "*Ouch!*"

"I'm telling you, these trees definitely *perambulate*," says Cyril ominously.

"Really?" says Lexi. "I think they just, like, walk around."

Jake grins at this. "Maybe you're both right," he says. "Ouch again! Something bit me." He glances down. A small shrub bares its teeth at him.

Lucas, in the lead, glances back nervously.

"Hey, guys, we *really* should have reached the perimeter fence by now," he says, pushing forward. "We didn't go the wrong way, did we?" As he says this, Lucas turns and slams into the perimeter fence. Holding his nose, he says, "And *that* hurt quite a bit."

"Great," says Cyril. He glances over at a couple of twisted, gnarly oaks. "If they smell blood, we're doomed." Cyril looks away from the oaks, then jerks his head to look back quickly. Both oaks pretend like they're just standing there.

Jake pats his brother's back. "You okay, man?"

"Yeah, I'm good," says Lucas, eyes watering.

"Let's get inside," says Jake. "Come on."

He leads the team along the security fence to an open entry gate.

Inside the perimeter fence sits a large, white-gray concrete building—the world-famous HQ of Team Spy Gear. As most of you know, this building is the abandoned "toy warehouse" of a company called Stoneship Toys. I put quotation marks around "toy warehouse" because, as Spy Gear fans know, no such toys ever existed. The toy company was a fiction, a front for a dark and deeply undercover spy organization known only as the Agency. Indeed, this warehouse is a highly sophisticated surveillance center filled with some of the most incredibly wicked spy gadgets you've ever seen.

Not far away, in a surveillance post hidden by a juniper thicket, a small man wearing a dark gray trench coat and black leather gloves watches our heroes troop into the warehouse yard.

The man rubs his gloved hands together. He sniffs the fine, scuffed glove leather.

He holds out his hands and flexes his fingers.

He gives the gloves a long, admiring appraisal.

But something coming through his Spy Link headset interrupts this activity. "Yes, Foxtrot Charlie here, I copy you, over." The Gloved Agent listens for a second, then barks, "Affirmative on that, Foxtrot One. The chicken is in the coop. Repeat, *The chicken is in the coop*, over."

He listens for a moment. As he does, he can't help himself; he has to hold out one gloved hand and make a fist. He points. Then he jabs his finger wildly, as if making a passionate point. As he does this, another trench-coated agent appears next to him.

"Sir?" says the new agent, a tall fellow.

A startled, high-pitched squeal escapes the Gloved Agent's mouth.

"Sorry, sir," says the tall agent.

The Gloved Agent clamps a hand over his Spy Link mouthpiece and barks, "What are you doing here, Agent Briggs?"

Briggs looks flustered. "I believe you sent for me, sir," he says.

The Gloved Agent sighs. He starts to speak, but then raises one finger dramatically—the classic "hold on just one minute" gesture—as he listens to another report in his ear. Finally, he says, "Roger that, Foxtrot Two. All units, stand by."

The Gloved Agent nods to Agent Briggs. "Report," he says wearily.

Briggs looks uncomfortable. "It's . . . bigger, sir," he says.

The Gloved Agent stares at him. "Bigger?" he says.

"Growing, sir," says Briggs. He lowers his voice. "Three hundred percent bigger than when we found the site just yesterday."

Now the Gloved Agent presses his hands together, as if praying. "My God," he says quietly.

Briggs nods. He says, "Units Victor and Zulu have secured a lockdown perimeter in the west woods, but, uh . . ." He hesitates a second.

"But what?" asks the Gloved Agent.

"Well, the guys are pretty nervous," says Briggs.

"Yes," says the Gloved Agent, looking grim, almost ill. "Yes, I'll wager they are."

Inside HQ, the team climbs ladder rungs recessed into the wall.

These lead up to a control room suspended over the main floor of the warehouse. As each kid reaches the open ceiling hatch, a huge, hairy hand reaches down to pull the climber through.

"Thanks, Marco," says Lexi as he swings her up into the control room.

Cyril plops into the leather captain's chair at the console. "Ah, home sweet home," he says. "Too bad this place is surrounded by homicidal foliage."

Marco folds his arms and stares at one of the side monitors, which displays a live video feed of a location in the woods.

"Something's going on," he says.

Jake and Lucas flank him at the monitor. "What is it?" asks Jake.

"I don't know," says Marco. "I caught movement from this Minicam. It's somewhere in the west woods." He shakes his shaggy head. "It was just a couple minutes ago. I also caught some coded chatter on one of my favorite channels." He looks down at Cyril. "Can I have my chair back, Sparky?"

Cyril stands up, bows, and steps aside.

Marco drops heavily into the chair and starts tapping on the keyboard at the main monitor. For those of you with no memory of previous Spy Gear books, perhaps because of their blinding literary brilliance, here's a quick look at the Stoneship HQ layout:

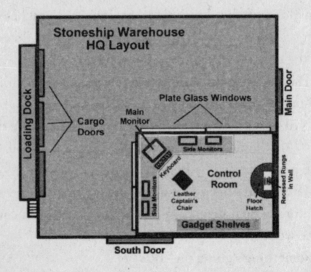

Stoneship Warehouse HQ Layout

Loading Dock

Cargo Doors

Main Monitor

Plate Glass Windows

Main Door

Side Monitors

Keyboard

Control Room

Side Monitors

Leather Captain's Chair

Floor Hatch

Recessed Rungs in Wall

Gadget Shelves

South Door

Lexi taps Marco on the shoulder. "What are you doing?" she asks.

"Drilling," says Marco.

Lucas watches Marco click the mouse and tap keys. Odd sounds crackle in the console speakers. Then he looks over at Lexi and says, "I think he's trying to hack into secure Agency com-link channels."

For a while, the kids watch Marco type and click with wizardly speed. Then, suddenly, he spins the chair around to face the kids.

"No holes today," says Marco angrily. He puts his hands on his knees, takes a deep breath, and then, after a long pause, says, "I hate it when I lose."

Jake sits down on the floor. "You'll feel better after you tell us everything," he says with a sly grin.

Marco says, "I doubt it."

The others sit too. Cyril lays back and puts his hands under his head.

"So," he says. "What-up, big dog?"

At this point we could go back and quickly review everything that happened the last time we saw Marco, back in Book 4: *The Doomsday Dust*. But, kids, let's not do that. Instead, let's pretend everybody just reread Book 4 and everything is incredibly fresh and clear in everybody's memory and therefore the author doesn't have to rehash who Marco is and why anybody cares what he's been doing for the past two months et cetera et cetera et cetera et cetera et cetera et cetera et cetera.

"Yes," says Lexi, noting the last paragraph. "Where have you been?"

"Uzbekistan," says Marco.

The kids start laughing. Marco just stares at them.

"Heh, heh!" chuckles Cyril. "Heh." He looks at Marco. "You're not kidding."

"No," says Marco.

"Uzbekistan?" says Lucas. "Wow. What were you doing in Uzbekistan?"

"Looking at scorch patterns," says Marco.

"Fun!" yells Cyril.

Marco ignores him and turns to the console. He types in a quick search string and brings up some images onscreen. Then he slides his chair back.

"Take a look," he says.

The kids approach and examine a set of photos on the main monitor. They show a dark, fractured cleft of rock, taken from different angles. Each photo is labeled TAKHTAKARACH PASS and numbered one through eight.

"What is it?" asks Jake.

"Well, one answer is, hey, it's a ravine," says Marco.

Jake turns to Marco. "And what's another answer?" he asks.

Marco clicks on one of the photos to zoom in on the view.

"A crash site," he says.

Jake leans in for a closer look at the blackened crevice. "Wow. And this is in Uzbekistan?"

"Yes," says Marco. "This crevice was torn out of a

remote mountain pass, about forty kilometers south of Samarkand."

"Ah yes, *Samarkand*." Cyril sighs.

Marco gives him a wary look. "You know Samarkand?"

"All too well."

Lucas rolls his eyes, then looks at Marco. "So what crashed?" he asks.

"Officially, it was a Class Two meteorite," says Marco.

"And unofficially—?" begins Lucas.

"Some sort of high-velocity . . . craft."

Now all four kids stare at Marco.

"A *craft*?" says Lucas, blinking.

"Well." Marco shrugs. "That's one theory, anyway."

"That's a heck of a theory," says Jake.

"It's a very popular one in the Agency right now," says Marco.

"Yes, *very* popular," hisses a deep, robotic voice.

Everyone spins toward this scary new voice. It comes from the open hatch that leads down to the warehouse floor. Moments later, a huge, dark apparition rises up through the hatch like a black angel.

Everybody screams, including the author.

Yes, you guessed it: He's back.

The Dark Man!

The Dark Man is a very high-level covert operative with the Agency. This massive fellow has been lurking on the murky fringes of Team Spy Gear's world for, let's see, almost five books now. Yes, for five long, brilliant, painstakingly crafted books, the towering, black-caped man has kept a close eye on the Bixbys and buddies in their galactic struggle against Viper. He's also knocked over a lot of stuff.

Cyril steps toward the huge man. "And so . . . we *meet again*," he intones.

The Dark Man plucks some leaves and small rodents off his cape. "I *hate* this forest," he rumbles in his deep, digitally altered voice.[11]

Cyril cups his hands over his mouth. "And what brings you to these parts, Dark Man?" he asks, fluttering his hands to make his voice wobble.

Lexi glances over at him. "What are you doing, Cyril?"

Cyril gives her a grim look. "I'm disguising my voice so nobody will recognize it later."

Lexi cracks up.

The Dark Man ignores this. He crosses the room and points to the photos on the main monitor. "So have the *children* come up with any new insight?" he asks Marco with a hint of sarcasm.

Marco is amused. "I'm sure they'll solve it for you." He pauses. "Again."

"Then you can get that big promotion to Executive Dark Man," says Cyril.

The Dark Man just looks at Cyril.

11. As most of you know, the Dark Man wears an LP voice-filter mask to warp his speech, making him sound a lot like Darth Vader's bassoon when he talks.

Jake leans in to examine the photos. "So what makes you think this ravine is an aircraft crash site?"

The Dark Man nods at Marco, who clicks on one of the photos to zoom in closer.

"The carbon scoring, for one," says Marco. On the close-up, he points to a dark spiral pattern on the rock face inside the cleft. "See that? It's *way* too symmetrical and perfect to be the result of, say, a meteorite hit. The Agency guys think it's some sort of nozzle exhaust residue."

Cyril looks closely. "Interesting," he says. "Why do we care?"

"An excellent question, Mr. Wong!" says the Dark Man very loudly.

Cyril starts nodding and waving to everybody.

"*Here's* why we care," says the Dark Man. "First, you should know that Viper has always been *extremely* tidy when he abandons a location." He turns to Marco, who nods in agreement. "He scours it clean, somehow . . . he sweeps away the tracks. We find *nothing* of value, *nothing* that might lead us to him. Nothing!" The Dark Man takes a deep breath; it sounds like radio static. "However," he continues, "we found one small item of interest when Viper made his hasty retreat from the nanotechnology lab in the old Blackwater mansion last February."[12]

The Dark Man nods at Marco, who taps a few keys on the keyboard. A map pops open onscreen.

12. See Book 4: *The Doomsday Dust.* After you see it, try actually *reading* it, will you?

"This map fragment was frozen in a scrambled data cluster on a handheld unit left behind," says the Dark Man. "Left by accident? Or just a clever bit of misdirection? We've analyzed it for months."

Lucas leans in close to the monitor. "Uzbekistan, I presume," he says.

"Exactly," rumbles the Dark Man. "The Kyrk-Tau region. Note the glowing yellow dot. That, of course, marks the exact location of the scorched rift that *some* believe is a crash site." He shakes his head slightly.

"You don't sound too convinced," says Jake.

"I'm not, yet."

"Here's where it gets weird," says Marco. "Kyrk-Tau is very unique, geographically speaking. Very heavily cratered. More than three thousand distinct craters, in all. Each one is filled with dozens if not hundreds of hidden grottoes, caves, chasms, clefts." He nods at the map. "It's the perfect location for, say . . . a hideout."

The Dark Man points at the map.

"Not far from the saddle of the Takhtakarach Pass is a truly stunning cavern nearly a full kilometer in length called Aman-Kutan," he says. "Some disturbing local legends have emerged over the past few years. Legends about people going into Aman Kutan and then coming out . . . changed."

"How so?" asks Jake.

"Well," says the Dark Man, "according to our *crack*

language experts"—he says this with a hint of sarcasm—"the best translation would be . . . 'possessed.'"

"Possessed?" says Lucas. "You mean, like, by demons?"

"Spirits," nods Marco. "Whatever."

"In any case, people behave very strangely after they exit the cave," explains the Dark Man. "They exhibit odd tics and twinges. And then, according to local sources, after a week, two weeks, these people leave town. They just . . . disappear."

Lexi suddenly jumps up. "Do they do this?" she asks.

She starts shrugging her shoulders up and down, repeatedly.

Cyril points at her and starts laughing. "That's hilarious!" he hoots.

But the Dark Man turns sharply toward Lexi. "Silence!" he orders, waving a hand at Cyril.

Cyril claps a hand over his mouth.

The Dark Man steps abruptly toward Lexi, who flinches. The contrast in their size is so striking, it looks like a Frankenstein monster looming over a rag doll. "*Where* did you see that, Miss Lopez?" he growls.

Lexi looks sheepish. "The beekeepers on the dock," she says.

The Dark Man swings his head toward Marco. "Shrugging beekeepers?" he snarls. "I saw *nothing* of this in your report!"

Lexi looks up fiercely. "Hey, I forgot to tell him about

it, so stop yelling." She seems to grow a few inches as she says this. The Dark Man actually takes a half step backward.

Marco grins. "Uh, yeah, what the tiny girl said," he says, gesturing at her.

"Speaking of the beekeepers," interjects Jake, "do you have any idea what was in that crate?"

"What crate?" asks the Dark Man.

"The containment chamber," says Marco. "I told you about that."

"Oh, right." The Dark Man hesitates.

"So what was it?" asks Lucas. "What's being 'contained'? It was definitely alive and sounded . . . really bad."

Jake notes the Dark Man's hesitance. "You sent your guys in there to investigate, right?"

"I'll field that one," says Marco. He stands up from the captain's chair and looks at Jake. "No," he says. Then he sits back down.

"No?" says Jake in disbelief, looking from Marco to the Dark Man. "You haven't busted AMBS yet?"

Marco sighs. "Think, Bixby," he says.

Jake folds his arms, thinking. Then he says, "You don't want to tip your hand yet. You want to spy on them a bit." He turns to the Dark Man. "You want to follow the trucks, right? The crate shipments? Because maybe they'll lead you to something bigger, more important."

Lucas raises his hand, jumping up and down. Everybody looks at him.

"Like maybe *Viper?*" he says excitedly.

The Dark Man suddenly reaches up to touch the Spy Link earpiece in his right ear.

"Yes, yes, I'm here," he says urgently. He dips his head, listening. After a few more seconds, he speaks quickly, and with a touch of anger. "Listen . . . *carefully*. Direct *all* units to fall back fifty yards, but maintain a perimeter. *Do not lose containment.* Understood? I'm on the way."

The Dark Man turns toward the floor hatch and grabs a ladder rung recessed in the wall.

"I must go," he says. "We have a situation in the woods, and my field commander is an idiot."

Lucas starts bouncing like a ball. "Need any help?" he asks. "We're excellent field agents."

"Right," says the Dark Man. He starts descending the rungs. "This is no place for children."

Lexi balls up her fists. "Why does everybody keep *calling* us that?"

Without another word, the Dark Man disappears. A few seconds later, a clatter rises up through the hatch, followed by a deep bellow and some bad words.

"That sounded pretty painful," says Cyril.

Jake is deep in thought. "Marco, I still don't get it

about the crash site," he says, glancing at the map on the monitor. "Do they think Viper crashed one of his aircraft in Uzbekistan, discovered a cave, and then decided to make it his base of operations?"

"No," says Marco.

The kids all look at him.

"So how about some answers, Mystery Dog," says Cyril.

Marco sits in the captain's chair and clicks back to the photos of the blackened ravine. "Look at that," he says. "Something hit so hard that it gouged a freaking crevice out of a solid granite dome, then exploded in a fireball so fierce, it coated the rock wall with a melted glaze." He looks at Jake. "Do you think any human being could survive such a thing?"

"No," says Jake. "Nothing could survive that."

"Well, let's hope so," says Marco.

"What do you mean?" asks Lucas.

Marco gazes at the photo set. "Because anything that could survive such an impact would be . . ." He doesn't finish the sentence.

"Inhuman?" says Lexi.

Marco just looks at her.

"So again, what does any of this have to do with Viper?" asks Jake.

"Who knows?" says Marco. "But that recovered map

from Blackwater suggests some kind of connection." He looks at Lexi again. "And your shrugging beekeepers sure got the big dude all worked up."

"Well, whatever's in that crate they delivered is also in the lagoon," says Cyril. "That shriek, man." He shivers. "It scared the left monkey out of me."

Jake grins. "What about the right monkey?"

"No, he's fearless."

Marco glances at his watch. "Crap!" he says. "I'm supposed to be at work in eight minutes." He hits a button to shut down the console.

"Okay, team, let's head home," says Jake. "But we need a plan of action."

"I think the plan is pretty obvious," says Cyril.

Jake gives him a look. "Really?"

Cyril leans in. "First, we lie low a few months," he says quietly. "And I mean *really* low." He bobs his head. "Then we move to Sweden."

"That's odd," says Lucas, rubbing his hands together. "I was thinking more along the lines of, like, two Go Teams operating under cover of darkness." He looks ecstatic. "This Friday night!"

Jake cracks a sly grin. "Yeah, one team can check out the local lagoon pumps," he says.

"And the other one can go for ice cream," says Marco as he disappears down the hatch.

"Exactly!" shouts Lucas.

Lexi, caught up in the excitement, says, "We have to wait till Friday?"

"It's the only night we can get out after dark," says Lucas.

Lexi nods. "True," she says. Then she looks wistful.

"What's wrong?" asks Lucas, seeing her look.

"It's going to be a *long* week," she says.

THAT THURSDAY

And boy, oh boy, what a *looooong* week it is.

Who would think that just one week could last so many days? Day after day, for *days*, Team Spy Gear waits for Friday evening to come. School, homework, saxophone lessons, family meals, and even sleep—it all drags on and on and on.

On Thursday, however, three things happen that actually make Thursday pretty interesting.

Right after school, Jake has soccer practice in Willow Park, directly across the street from school. Afterward, he juggles a ball, waiting for Cyril. The plan is for the guys to study together that evening for a brutal Math Difficulties test.

As Jake flicks the ball upward again and again, he

notices the back of a purple head on a park bench facing away from him. He catches the ball and moves closer. Sure enough, it's Barbie Bickle. She's reading a slender book of poetry.

As he watches her read, Jake suddenly knows what he must do.

"Hey," says Jake.

Barbie turns to stare at him. After a long moment, she says, "You look familiar."

"I'm in Mrs. Porkbat's Language Arts class," says Jake. "I sit in the back." He jerks his thumb over his shoulder. "Like, way back behind you. *Way* back."

"I'm kidding, Bixby," says Barbie.

"Oh," says Jake. "Heh. Well."

Barbie closes her book. Then she stares off into the distance.

After a couple of weeks, Jake clears his throat. Then he says, "I, uh, wanted to ask you something."

Barbie gives him a suspicious look. "About what?"

"About your poem."

"What poem?"

Jake frowns. "The one you read in class?"

Barbie's eyes darken. "Why?"

"Uh, because I . . ."

"I don't trust you, Bixby," interrupts Barbie.

Jake is flabbergasted. "Why not?" he asks.

"Because you . . ." begins Barbie. But then she stops.

She glances down at her book, thinking. The silence is long, and feels like something you could grab and shake. Then she looks back up at Jake; she stares hard, as if peering inside of him, which is something *I'd* never do because I'm afraid of seeing people's guts and stuff, but enough about me. After a long, probing look, Barbie finally says, "What about the poem?"

Jake grips the back of the bench. "Whew! Well, uh, for one, it scared the holy living crab legs right out of me."

Now Barbie looks bitterly amused. She says, "Hey, I'm Psycho Chick."

Aha! thinks Jake.

You see, Psycho Chick is the nickname many kids at Carlos Santana Middle School have bestowed upon Barbie Bickle. It started (like most mean things at Santana) with the Wolf Pack, a bunch of bullies led by the alpha bully, Brill Joseph. Then it was taken up by the Flesh-Eaters, the mean-girl equivalent of the Wolf Pack. Soon it was a common name.

Jake nods. *"That's* why you don't trust me," he says. "You think I'm like everybody else."

Barbie says, *"Everybody* is."

"Everybody is what?"

"Like everybody else."

"You don't trust *anybody*?" asks Jake.

"No," says Barbie.

Astounded by this, Jake walks around the bench and

plops down next to Barbie. This maneuver makes her sit up very straight and stare at him. He tosses the soccer ball lightly a few times; then he turns toward her dark, startled eyes.

"I'm not like everybody else," he says.

Barbie just looks at him.

Then Jake asks: "Did you actually see the thing?"

Now Barbie looks away and says, "It's just a poem, Bixby."

But Jake is not convinced. "Hey," he says. "You know my friend Cyril? Cyril Wong?"

Barbie's head is still turned away, but she slides her eyes sideways to peek at Jake. She says, "The kid with the hair."

"Yeah, that's the one."

"So?" asks Barbie.

Jake leans toward her. "He saw it too."

Barbie looks at the grass for a second. Then she looks at Jake and says, "The Black Hand?"

"Yes," says Jake. "In the water."

"Where?" asks Barbie.

"In the golf lagoon," says Jake. "Is that where you saw it?"

Barbie looks stunned. "Yes," she says.

Jake jumps up. "Whoa!" he shouts. "Ha! *Wooo!*" He punches the air. Then: "Whoa. Wait." He turns to Barbie. "You're not a golfer, too, are you?"

"No," says Barbie.

"Then how did you . . . ?" begins Jake.

"I sneak onto the course after dark and sit by the lagoon." She gives Jake a grim look. "I usually find it very relaxing."

"But on the night in question, it probably wasn't very relaxing," says Jake, grinning.

A thin smile flickers on Barbie's lips.

"Actually, there were two nights in question," she says.

An hour later, Cyril still can't believe it.

"You *talked* to Barbie Bickle," he says. "How could that be?"

"It's a stunning development," agrees Jake.

"I'll say," says Cyril.

Jake pulls out a folded sheet of journal paper from his pocket.

"Here's the map she made," he says. He unfolds it and flattens it out on the tabletop. "The Long Lagoon," he says. "There. She marked the two locations where she observed odd activity."

"Excellent!" says Cyril. "Now we have something to throw darts at while we're lying low."

Jake grins. "Or we could use it when you and I deploy to the golf course tomorrow night."

Cyril nods bleakly. "I don't like night, Jake," he says. "It scares me."

"I know," says Jake.

"Cat, on the other hand, really enjoys sneaking around in the dark," says Cyril.

"Hmmm," says Jake. "Maybe we should ask her to join us."

Cyril brightens. "Hey, yeah!" he says. "Then she could watch my back while you take the lead."

"What about peril that approaches from the sides?" asks Jake.

Cyril rubs his chin. "Right," he says. "I forgot about that."

Jake opens his Math Difficulties textbook to the Chapter 13 Review and looks down at it. "Dude, I'm gonna find it very hard to study tonight," he says. "I'm a little excited."

"Math is life, Jake," says Cyril.

"Okay," says Jake. He reads the first chapter-review question: "'What's the square root of Bob Stevens?'" He looks at Cyril. "Wow, I'm stumped already."

Cyril whips out a calculator and taps a few buttons.

Both boys gaze at the answer.

"Wow, I never would have guessed *that*," says Jake.

Jake's cell phone rings. He flips it open and looks at the incoming number. Then he smiles and puts the phone to his ear.

"Hey, ice-cream man," he says.

"I'm in the backyard," says Marco over the phone.

"Here?" says Jake. "At Cyril's?"

"Yes."

"We'll be right down," Jake says, and snaps shut the phone. He looks at Cyril. "Marco's in your backyard."

Cyril nods. "That explains all the gnawed chicken bones I've been finding back there."

Jake laughs. The boys bound downstairs from Cyril's room and out the back door.

"Over here," calls a deep voice.

Marco steps out from the shadows under an apple tree. As you might have guessed, this is the second interesting thing that happens.

"What's up?" asks Jake.

"Dark matter," says Marco.

"No kidding!" says Cyril. "Me too!"

Marco gives him a hard look. "I thought you were such a research beast," he says.

"I am," says Cyril. "I'm *money*, baby. When it comes to search engines and the like, anyway."

"So what did you find on those Omega Link messages you got?" asks Marco.

"You mean the wimps and macho stuff?" asks Cyril.

"Yes," says Marco.

"Well, I'll tell you," replies Cyril. "If you give me five dollars."

"No, I'll tell *you* and save my money," says Marco, glancing behind him toward the trees. "You found a link to dark matter."

"Actually, little Bixby found that link," says Cyril. "I must give credit where credit is due."

Jake glances over at the trees too. "I thought nobody knows what dark matter is."

"Exactly," says Marco, gesturing up at the sky. "Physicists

can't even find it out there. It's theoretical. Calculations tell them dark matter has to exist, but nobody really knows. Is it invisible somehow? Is it in big clumps, like black holes? Or is it in particles so small, we can't detect them?" Marco shrugs. "Or maybe all of the above. We have no clue."

Cyril suddenly slaps at a mosquito. The crack is loud and makes Marco start.

"Jumpy?" asks Cyril, grinning.

Marco nods. "I think I'm being followed," he says.

"Tonight?" asks Jake, looking around.

"Just in general," says Marco.

Cyril guffaws. "Why would they follow *you?*" he asks. "To get free ice cream?"

Marco sighs. "Gotta go," he says. He turns toward the trees again. "Keep nosing around this dark matter thing. The spooks think something's there."

"The Agency?" asks Jake, surprised.

"Yeah," says Marco. "Dark matter science is a very, very weird area." As he walks away across the yard, he adds, "And I don't like it."

Meanwhile, just blocks away, the third interesting thing is about to happen. It starts when Lucas seizes a stuffed duck and peeks over the top of a beanbag chair. Across the room, something moves.

He zings the duck.

"Eat fluffy death!" he screams to the enemy.

Lexi laughs like a brutal dictator gone mad with unchecked power. "Dude, you didn't even hit my *zip code*," she guffaws.

Lucas reaches down for another duck, but finds nothing. "What, no ammo?" he gasps in pathetic desperation. "How can this be?"

"Oh, it *be*," yells Lexi.

She leaps up from her blast bunker and raises two lobsters over her head. "Die!" she howls, and charges across the bedroom, flinging crustaceans.

"I'm hit!" screams Lucas, holding his shoulder. He collapses to the ground. *"Medic!"*

Hey, after almost two freaking hours of homework, you'd be tossing lobsters too. As Lexi approaches the wounded Lucas, he suddenly grabs a foam centipede and starts beating her ankles viciously. In an astonishing evasive maneuver, Lexi dolphin-dives over the arthropod and rolls under her bed.

Then she hears it: *Beep!*

"What's that?" she calls.

Lucas doesn't answer. She hears him scrambling.

Beep!

"Is it the *thing*?" she calls.

"Yes!" shouts Lucas.

Lexi is wary, which is something a good spy should always be. But then she hears a familiar clanking: Lucas is digging in his gadget backpack. She scoots out from under the bed in time to see him hold up the Omega Link display screen.

"It's gone mad," he says, frowning.

"Let me see," says Lexi.

Lucas turns the screen toward her. It reads:

FLUSH THE MANTIS

"Whoa," she says, taking the Omega Link.

"Yes," agrees Lucas. "Whoa."

"That's insane."

"It's monkeys."

"What's it mean?" asks Lexi.

"You're the code breaker," says Lucas. "You tell me."

"Flush the mantis?" says Lexi. She shrugs.

Lucas whips the Spy Gear Casebook out of his backpack and opens it. Lexi tosses him a pen from her work desk. He jots the new message in the book. Then he looks up at Lexi and sighs.

"Dude, we need a team meeting," he says.

Beep!

"Oh, no," says Lexi. She holds up the display. "Not again."

Lucas jumps beside her, and they watch the previous message disappear. Then, with another beep, a new message begins. This one appears letter by letter, as if being typed:

ANTIGRAV CONTAINME

But as the last letter—the "E"—appears, the device beeps again, and the message disappears.

"Gadzooks!" yells Lucas.

"Quick! Write it down!" says Lexi.

Just as Lucas finishes jotting down the aborted message, the Omega Link emits yet another beep. A whole message pops onto the screen.

This one reads:

DISREGARD NONSENSE STRING

Beep! It disappears.

Lucas scribbles furiously.

"Get it all down!" says Lexi.

"I got it, I got it!" says Lucas. "'Disregard nonsense string,'" right?"

"Yes," nods Lexi.

Beep! Beep! Beep!

Suddenly, a string of characters and numbers start flowing across the screen. *Beep!* They disappear. *Beep!* They start up again.

"Holy dog biscuits," murmurs Lucas, watching.

Lexi jabs the Omega Link at Lucas. He grabs and holds it at arm's length, half afraid to set it down, but half afraid to keep holding it. Do the math: That adds up to one whole afraid.

Beep! The nonsense string disappears again.

There is a long pause.

"Is it *done* now, do you think?" asks Lucas.

Lexi sees his unease. She takes the device, listens to it, shakes it a little, then sets it down on the desktop.

"I guess," she says. "Wow."

Beep!

With big eyes, Lucas and Lexi lean over the Omega Link and read the new message.

PLEASE

With a beep, it disappears. Then, one more beep, and one last message.

It reads:

HELP ME, BIXBYS

Guess what, kids?

Looking into the future, the author can officially tell you that this is the last Omega Link message that Team Spy Gear will ever receive.

8

IN RELATED MATTERS

Friday evening, 8 p.m. . . . yeah, finally! Time for some *spy action*!

But wait, who's that?

Hey, *that's* not Team Spy Gear! That guy with the gaucho hat, hunched over a computer keyboard, is Dr. Tim, owner of Native Care Solutions Inc., and bona fide environmental wacko scientist.

On the desk next to his computer is a small glass jar of water. Inside the jar, one small, buglike entity swims around lazily. Dr. Tim grabs the jar, looks closely at the bug, then sets it down and types something.

Let's move the camera over his shoulder so we can see, shall we?

He types in the words "amphibious insect" and clicks a search button.

A short list of links appears: only three, in fact. He clicks on the first link. The homepage of a company website appears. The logo at the top of the screen reads:

AMBS Inc.
AmphiModular
BioSystems

But the only text on the page below it reads **Document no longer exists**.

Dr. Tim tries clicking on various links in the AMBS website, but finds that all articles and other documents have been deleted.

Why didn't they just take down the entire website? he wonders.

Then Dr. Tim opens a separate window to another page that reads: **U.S. Government Restricted**.

You may recall that Dr. Tim once worked for a very high-level government laboratory. Back then, he often searched through classified scientific databases with a powerful government search engine known only as [CENSORED BY THE CIA]. Old friends who still work at the lab regularly give Dr. Tim the latest passwords for this search engine.[13]

He uses one now to access [CENSORED BY THE CIA].

He types "amphibious insects" again. This time, only one result appears.

13. I'd tell you their names, but then very large men in black cars would visit you, plus I don't want to end up in a dungeon.

Dr. Tim opens the document. It's a scientific article describing a study linked to government-sponsored research of ant colony behavior. Here, a team of scientists traveled worldwide to investigate reports of rare ant species that could survive underwater.

The results were disappointing.

The first amphibious ant proved to be nothing more than a species of "skating ants"—ants that had developed the ability to scoot across water without breaking the surface tension. The team tracked this species to the tidal mangroves of tropical Australia.

After that, the scientists made trips to South Asia, Mexico, and regions of the Amazon, each time finding that the "fish-ant" of local legend proved to be nonexistent or else some other species of aquatic insect that spent only its larval stages underwater.

The team was disbanded shortly after one final trip, more than five years ago. It yielded more disappointing results, so the project was finally laid to rest with the publication of this summary report.

That final trip was to Uzbekistan.

Go Team One

Night has fallen, but the full moon is so bright that Jake, Cyril, and Cat watch their shadows creep ahead of them on the faded gray asphalt of Route 36. Cyril has mixed feelings about this.

"Guys, I like moonlight," he says. "But I swear"—he lowers his voice to a whisper—"my shadow keeps glaring back at me."

Cat is amused. "He's wondering if he can count on you for backup," she says.

"Oh, yeah?" says Cyril. "Well, whenever I really need *him*—like, in a dark room—he just *disappears*." He points down at their three shadows, which do seem to slink along somewhat suspiciously now. "Look at them! How do we know they haven't cut a deal with the bad guys?" He slogs along grumpily. "And here we are, just following them like fools."

Jake raises his hand for a halt.

"Okay, guys," he says. "Let's gear up."

Cat looks at him. "What do you mean?"

Jake reaches into a huge pocket of his cargo pants and pulls out three pairs of Spy Mission Gloves. He hands a pair to Cat, then to Cyril. He grins and adds, "If we don't use these, Lucas will be very disappointed."

"Gee, we don't want that," mumbles Cyril.

Cat looks down at hers. "Cool," she says. "What do they do?"

Jake slips one on. The "glove" is actually a soft plastic strap that slides over the pointing finger and then fastens around the wrist.[14]

"This one has signal lights for silent nighttime

14. You can see the Spy Mission Gloves on the cover of this book. But remember, it's just a picture. Please don't try to wear the book cover on your hands.

communication," says Jake. He presses a switch by his wrist; a red beam shoots out. "Red means stop immediately, imminent danger," he adds. "Yellow means caution, hold on. Green of course means all clear, proceed as planned."

Now Jake straps on the other glove unit. Cat and Cyril do likewise.

"This one's different," says Cat.

"It's a voice recorder," explains Jake. "If you want to make note of something in the dark, just hold down the red button and talk into the mike." He holds the glove up to his mouth and tries it. "Testing, testing, one two three." Then he plays the message back.

"Slick stuff," says Cat.

"Good for spying in the dark," says Jake.

The trio approaches the fence of the Carrolton Municipal Golf Course. Its chain-link fence looms like a webbed nightmare.

"Well, here we are," says Cat.

"Yes," says Cyril. "The Border of Insanity."

Cat glances at him. "Part of me wants to find The Black Hand," she says. "And part of me doesn't."

"Which part doesn't?" asks Cyril. "Because that's my favorite part."

Cat ignores him and unfolds the sheet of paper she's been carrying. It's Barbie Bickle's map. She squints at it in the moonlight. "So . . . Psycho Chick saw something under the Swilken Burn footbridge, eh?" she says.

"Hey . . . ," begins Jake. But then he hesitates.

Cat looks at him. "What?" she says.

"Don't . . . uh, don't call her that," says Jake.

"Psycho Chick?" asks Cat.

"Right," says Jake.

Cat gives him an amused look. "Okay, Bixby," she says. "Whatever." She squints at the map again. As Jake hands her a small mini-light, she adds, "I've always found it pretty spooky . . . the bridge, that is."

"Why?" asks Jake.

"It's kind of dark and secluded," says Cat. She shines the red mini-light on the map. "It's a replica of the famous stone footbridge over the Swilken Burn at St. Andrews Old Course," she says. "Very famous in golf. They play the British Open there regularly."

Cyril suddenly interrupts. "And *where* . . . is St. Andrews Old Course?" he asks.

"Scotland," answers Cat.

Cyril gulps. "Scotland?"

"Yeah," says Cat.

Cyril nods grimly. "Of course," he says gravely. "All the pieces fit so nicely."

Cat frowns. "What do you mean?"

Cyril gives her a significant look. "When you think of Scotland, *what* comes to mind?" asks Cyril.

Cat thinks for a second. "Bagpipes?" she says.

"No!" says Cyril.

"Guys in skirts?" asks Cat.

"Wrong again!"

Jake pulls a Spy Walkie Talkie out of another pocket in his pants. "Uh, Cyril's pretty sure The Black Hand is actually the Loch Ness monster," he says. He pushes the call button. "Loch Ness, as you know, Cat, is in Scotland."

"Ahhh," says Cat, nodding. "Got it."

Cyril gives her a wary look. "You're going to mock me now, right?" he says.

"Right," says Cat, grinning.

Go Team Two here, crackles the voice of Lucas from the walkie-talkie. This is Lima Bravo. Is that you, Go Team One, over?

"Yeah, dude, it's me," says Jake into the talkie. "We're at the golf fence, and we're going in, over."

Roger that, One, replies Lucas. We are at rendezvous point India Charlie, waiting for Mike Romeo. Assume all systems go for your maneuver, over.

"Marco's not there yet?" asks Jake with concern.

Ah, no, not yet, One, says Lucas. But Lima Lima just completed cell phone telecom contact with that unit, and he'll be here in five, over.

"Okay," says Jake, relieved. "I don't want you two going into that yard alone. It's bad enough that we're disobeying Agency orders by doing our own spying. I don't want trouble."

We wouldn't be going in alone, says Lexi's voice suddenly. There's, like, two of us.

"Right," says Jake, grinning. "You know what I mean."

Affirmative, says Lucas. We're little kids, over.

"That's a big *double*-roger on that," says Jake.

Cyril taps his arm. "Jake," he says, "there's no such thing as a 'big double-roger.'" He thinks for a second. "Except maybe for pirates. But, no, that would be a big double *jolly* roger."

"Whatever," says Jake. Into the talkie, he says, "Don't go in without Marco!"

We won't, says Lexi.

"Promise?"

Promise.

"Okay, guys, good luck," says Jake. "Eyes open, mouths shut."

Got it, says Lucas. Say, you've all mounted your SMGs, haven't you, Go Team One?

"Yes," says Jake, giving Cat an amused look. She rolls her eyes. Cyril suddenly seizes the walkie-talkie from Jake and speaks into it. "Roger that, Lima Bravo, we have Spy Mission Glove payload at zero niner-niner seven, mounted and ready for surveillance-level, voiceless, LED, signal-com orbital trajectory, over?"

There is static for a few seconds.

Then Lucas says, Right. Lexi's voice can be heard in the background saying, What the donkey is he talking about? Lucas answers, Cyril's just . . . kidding. After a second, Lexi's voice says, Oh.

"Hey, over there!" hisses Cat suddenly.

She grabs each boy by the arm and drags them both down behind a bush.

"What is it?" whispers Jake, crouching. He quickly shuts off his walkie-talkie unit.

"Up the fence line," whispers Cat.

The three peer over the top of the shrub. Not far away, about forty yards or so, a pair of figures approaches the golf course fence. It looks like two men, both dressed in light-colored jumpsuits. When they reach the fence, they look around, surveying the area. Then both grab hold of the chain-link fence and clamber over, dropping onto the golf course.

Jumpsuits glowing in the moonlight, the men drift across the fairway. They disappear into the pine trees on the opposite side.

"They're heading for the lagoon," says Cat.

"Let's go!" says Jake.

Cyril sighs.

The three kids hop the fence and glide quietly across the fairway grass.

Go Team Two

Lucas and Lexi lean against the wall in front of Ye Olde Ice-Cream Shoppe. Headlights approach. The vehicle's muffler rumbles loudly.

"That's him!" cries Lexi.

Sure enough, a decrepit silver Mazda chugs into a parking spot on the street. Marco emerges from the car and hurries over to them.

"Sorry I'm late," he says. "But I had a hunch about something and did a little research." He eyes Lucas. "Plus I brought you these."

He hands Lucas two pod-shaped gadgets.

Lucas is ecstatic. "What are they?" he asks, holding them up reverently.

"It's a handheld mobile tracking device called an Agent Tracker," says Marco. "You put that bug on something, and then use the handheld seeker unit to track it down. Put them in your backpack."

As Lucas does so, Marco crouches down to Lexi's eye level. "And I've got some news," he says.

"About Viper?" she asks.

"No, about you," says Marco. "And, well . . . me."

Lexi frowns. "What is it?"

Marco sticks out his huge hand. Lexi absently takes it in hers. Marco pumps her hand twice.

"Congratulations," he says. "We're related."

Lexi just stares at him.

"Are you kidding?" says Lucas.

"No, I'm not." Marco stands up.

Lexi blinks, trying to digest this information. Then she says, "But your name is Rossi."

"What's your mom's maiden name?" asks Marco.

"Santiago," says Lexi.

"Did she ever talk about her cousin Alicia? Alicia Santiago?"

Lexi thinks. Then she says, "Do people call her Lissie?"

"They do," says Marco.

"Yeah, I remember the name. What about her?"

"She's my mother," says Marco.

"Wow!" shouts Lucas. He slaps Lexi's back. "That's incredible! That's awesome!"

The roar of a gunning truck engine suddenly rises from behind the store.

"And *that's* our cue," says Marco. He looks over at Lucas, who slings his gadget backpack over both shoulders and tightens the waist strap. Then Marco quickly opens the back hatch of his Mazda and slides out a collapsible Fiberglas ladder.

"Wow," says Lucas, watching this. He shakes his head and looks over at Lexi. "Cousins!"

Lexi is now smiling big. "Ha!" is all she can say. And then "Ha!" again.

"Let's move," says Marco. "We don't want to miss that truck."

The threesome hurries down the side alley. Marco hoists the ladder over the four-foot chain-link fence and drops it gently on the other side. They all quickly climb over. Marco unfolds the ladder—it now extends ten feet—and tilts it against the tall wooden fence along the back alley behind the ice-cream shop. He climbs until he can peek over the top.

"What's going on?" whispers Lucas.

Marco waves his hand for silence. Then, after a few more seconds, he descends.

"They're loading something onto a truck," he says.

"What is it?"

"Looks like a coffin," says Marco. "Must be another containment chamber."

"Or maybe the same one," says Lucas.

"We need to track it," says Marco.

Both guys turn to look at Lexi.

Lexi grins big. She holds out her hand. "Bug, please," she says.

Lucas digs the bug unit out of his bag and gives it to her. "You so *go*, girl," he says.

Marco reaches out and grabs her shoulder. "Don't take risks," he says. "There's a lot of activity on the dock." He taps the bug in her hand. "Hook it under the front bumper and get out *fast*."

Lexi pats Marco's hand. "No worries," she says.

And in two seconds she's up the ladder and over the fence.

The white pickup truck rumbles down Ridgeview Drive as it curves past the lakefront houses on Carrolton Reservoir's east shore. At Platte Park, the housing ends. Here, Ridgeview Drive runs a mere twenty feet from the water's edge.

The truck stops in the park. Dr. Tim gets out.

He strides toward the reservoir carrying a notebook, a lit flashlight, and a bamboo pole.

At the water's edge, he aims the flashlight beam down into the depths. Carrolton Reservoir is very clean, thanks to a system of filtration pumps installed by the city. So Dr. Tim's flashlight clearly reveals the bottom, out to almost thirty feet. Dr. Tim walks along slowly, examining the reservoir floor, stopping occasionally to stoop and look closer.

Then, suddenly, he stops. He trains the beam on an underwater bump about the size of a pumpkin. In fact, it kind of *looks* like a pumpkin too. A pumpkin with a hole on top.

Dr. Tim crouches. He opens up his notebook with one hand and reads something he wrote earlier. He nods.

Then he turns the page.

There, a photocopied article is pasted in. It looks like

some fun reading. The title is "Bottom-Sediment Core Samples in the Charvak Reservoir, Chirchik River, Uzbekistan." The article, which is very technical, describes how a team of Russian scientists discovered some strange, hivelike structures in the floor of a man-made lake in Uzbekistan. These underwater colonies were abandoned by whatever built them.

Photos at the bottom of the article show one of these odd hives.

Hey, it looks like a pumpkin with a hole on top.

Now Dr. Tim drops the notebook and wields his bamboo pole. He dips it in the water and jabs it into the colony. Small, insectlike creatures suddenly spew from the new hole. Some of them cling to the pole. Dr. Tim pulls it out of the water and trains the light on the creatures. Yep, they're the very same eight-legged, antlike bugs he found in Ted Barky's yard and Jack Barge's garden.

"Interesting," says Dr. Tim.

The bugs quickly swarm around the pole, crawling around and around in a tight ring about halfway down its shaft.

As Dr. Tim guides the light along the pole, the beam hits the water again, illuminating the hive. Suddenly, the top of the hive bursts open. A much larger creature emerges, with sediment swirling all around it. It pulses in place for a second, then scuttles away on multiple legs, like a crab.

"A crab?" murmurs Dr. Tim. "Maybe that's the hive queen."

He drops his bamboo pole in the grass and follows the leggy entity, keeping the flashlight on it. But it moves so fast, it soon loses him.

"That's no crab," says Dr. Tim.

Rubbing his chin in thought, he slowly saunters back to his notebook and pole. When he trains his flashlight on them, Dr. Tim sees that the insects are gone.

And the bamboo pole has been snapped in half.

9

DOWN THE HATCH

Hey, things are getting pretty exciting, eh?

I mean, just a few pages ago everybody was doing homework, for gosh sakes. People were studying *math*. Now here we are, spying and following scary men.

Frankly, I'm a little nervous about what I'm about to write next.

I just hope it doesn't get all bloody and stuff.

Go Team One

The Long Lagoon looks alive under the full moon. Reflected light wriggles across its surface.

The two men in jumpsuits stand motionless at the water's edge. Neither one speaks. For a minute or so, it is very, very quiet.

Crickets chirp. The breeze takes a few light breaths.

Water gently laps the shore.

Then a bubbling sound, followed by a loud, wet snort, rises above the night's murmurs. It comes from somewhere up the shoreline.

The two men jerk their heads to look.

Not far from the men, hidden by pine branches, Jake turns to Cyril and Cat.

It's Bixby decision time!

First, Jake points at himself, then points toward the snorting sound. (Meaning: *I'll go check it out.*) Next, Jake points at both Cyril and Cat, then points at the ground. (Meaning: *You guys stay here.*) Finally, Jake cooks up some pork chops. (Meaning: *The author is insane.*) No, actually, Jake slides silently behind the pine trees toward a rustic stone footbridge.

You guessed it: That's the Swilken Burn bridge.

As Jake approaches it, another loud snort makes him freeze.

A jet of water shoots out from under the bridge.

What the heck? thinks Jake.

The bubbling sounds continue. Jake creeps closer.

The Swilken Burn footbridge is just wide enough for a golf cart. It spans a narrow stretch of the lagoon, connecting the nearby green to the next hole's tee. The asphalt path to the bridge is lined with azalea bushes in full bloom, flowers pale in the moonlight. Jake crouches behind them and follows the path.

When he reaches the lagoon's edge, Jake stares down

under the bridge. One spot appears to be . . . boiling? The black water bubbles; it swirls into whirlpools. This eerie, turbulent circle emerges and starts moving slowly along the shoreline.

Jake, mesmerized by the odd sight, creeps out of the bushes. He glances up ahead . . . and suddenly notices two red LED lights flashing at him from the pine trees.

He looks down at his gloves.

Uh-oh, he remembers, *red means danger*.

Jake dives back behind the azaleas just as the two men in jumpsuits round the clump of trees up ahead. *Whew!* Close one! Then he peeks over the bushes to see a very disturbing sight.

The men walk like zombies toward him.

The water turbulence—the bubbles—moves ominously toward them, then stops near the shore.

The men stop too. One steps onto the water. Yes, "onto" the water. Meaning: He walks across the water's surface toward the bubbles.

Jake, stunned, rises from the bushes.

When the man reaches the boiling spot, water suddenly whooshes up all around him. Then he sinks quickly, as if sucked downward.

Now the second man walks across the water.

Jake can't help it. "No!" he shouts. "*No!*"

But with a whoosh, the second man is sucked under the rippling surface.

Up ahead, Cat and Cyril burst from the trees.

"My God!" shouts Cyril. "It *ate* them!"

Go Team Two

Marco, standing atop the Fiberglas stepladder, leans his massive body over the fence. From below, where Lucas stands, he looks like a big pair of legs missing the top half of its body.

"Where is she?" whispers Lucas. "Where's Lexi?"

Marco's upper torso and head reappear for a second. "It's all good," he says quietly, "but climb up and hang on to my feet, will you? Just in case?"

Lucas scrambles up the ladder under Marco as the big man hangs back over the fence. As Lucas hugs Marco's feet, he hears scrabbling sounds on the opposite side of the wooden fence, moving upward. Then he looks up to see Marco yank Lexi over the fence top with one hand.

"Down, Bixby!" hisses Marco.

Lucas hops to the ground. Marco swings Lexi around and below him, where she latches on to the ladder and climbs down. Then Marco follows.

As Marco quickly collapses and refolds the ladder, they hear the truck gun its engine loudly on the other side of the fence. Gears grind, then the delivery vehicle roars again.

"There he goes," says Lucas.

"Turn on the tracker!" says Lexi, excited.

Lucas digs the Agent Tracker seeker unit out of his hip pocket and turns it on.

"To the car!" says Marco. "Hustle."

The threesome hurries down the alley to Marco's Mazda, hops inside, and fastens seat belts. Marco fires up the car as Lucas holds up the seeker unit. Gazing at the tracker's color-coded indicators, Lucas barks orders to Marco, guiding him to the AMBS truck. It doesn't take long to fall in behind the bugged delivery vehicle; when they lose sight of it after getting caught at red lights, the seeker unit quickly gets them back on track.

After ten minutes of driving, the Mazda ends up parked (headlights off) on the side of County Road 44 where it runs along Stoneship Woods. Up ahead about a hundred yards, the AMBS truck backs off the road into the trees.

"What are they doing?" asks Lucas. "There's no road there."

"Let's go," says Lexi, leaning forward. "Let's get in there! Let's check it out!"

"Easy there, Spunky," says Marco. He brings a pair of night-vision binoculars to his eyes. "Okay, looks like three delivery men. Same beekeeper suits." He adjusts the scope. "And they're unloading a crate."

"Let's go," says Lexi.

Lucas pulls out his own night-scope and trains it on the truck down the road.

"Boy, they look nervous," he says.

Marco nods. "They're handling that crate very carefully," he agrees.

"Whoa!" says Lucas, staring through the scope. "Do you see that?"

Marco frowns. He leans out the side window for a cleaner view. "That's a forklift," he says.

"It just, like, popped out of the bushes!" says Lucas.

Lexi can't stand it anymore. She dives headfirst out of the window, tucks into a perfect forward somersault, and pops up. Then she approaches the window and leans into the car.

"Let's go," she says.

Lucas nods, impressed. "Let's go," he says.

Marco quietly opens his door. "Yeah," he says. "Let's go."

Ten minutes later, Lucas and Marco crouch under a tall cottonwood tree in the heart of Stoneship Woods. It is very, very dark here; no moonlight penetrates the evil canopy of this forest. Fortunately, both fellows wear Spy Night Patrol-Listeners—night vision goggles with attached listening devices.

Above them, branches shiver lightly. Marco and Lucas look up.

A small body suddenly drops from the tree. It lands between them. Guess who?

"It opens up," whispers Lexi, pointing ahead. "And there's light."

"Light?" repeats Marco.

Lexi nods, her spy goggles jiggling. "Red light," she says.

Both guys stand up. For the last ten minutes, the trio has

been following the rumble of a forklift down a newly cut trail through the woods. Seconds ago, the forklift stopped up ahead, so the team sent Lexi to do some vertical reconnaissance.[15] As everybody knows, *nobody* does vertical reconnaissance quite as beastly good as Lexi Lopez.

Marco leads the way down the trail. "So there's a clearing?" he asks.

"I guess," says Lexi.

"How far ahead?" asks Lucas, walking beside her.

"Maybe fifty or sixty trees," she answers.

Marco turns to look at her. "You measure distance in trees?" he asks.

Lexi shrugs. "In a forest," she says.

Marco turns and trudges forward. "Good point," he says.

Lucas grins and follows.

The night-vision goggles give everyone a clear vision of the path ahead. After about thirty-eight and a half trees, Marco stops. He pulls off his goggles. So do Lucas and Lexi.

A faint red glow filters through the foliage up ahead.

"Pack the goggles," says Marco.

He and Lexi hand their headsets to Lucas, who stows all three in his gadget backpack. Sure enough, the red light grows more intense as they creep farther down the trail. Then they hear the hydraulic sound of the forklift's fork.

"They must be lowering the crate," whispers Lucas.

15. Also known as "spying from trees."

Marco surges ahead. "We need to see what's in that containment chamber," he says. As he moves forward, his figure becomes a huge, shaggy silhouette ringed by a chilling red glow.

Lucas and Lexi follow.

Seconds later, they reach a low stand of wild boxwood on the fringe of a red-lit clearing. Above, a towering bank of spotlights masked in red lighting gel illuminates the area.

Marco, Lexi, and Lucas peek over the boxwoods.

A huge, grooved mound of dirt rises nearly ten feet high on the far side of the clearing. Next to it, four "bee-keepers" slide a coffin-shaped crate off the steel forks of the lift truck. They set it at the base of the mound.

"Holy Pop-Tarts," whispers Lucas.

"It looks like a huge . . . pumpkin," whispers Lexi, staring at the mound.

Indeed, it does. Evenly spaced grooves rise up its rounded sides. The open area around it looks recently cleared; pale stumps and fresh-cut branches lie scattered at the edges of the clearing. Bathed in the red light, everything looks very . . . alien.

Marco doesn't speak. But he looks grim, very grim.

Lucas slides along the boxwoods, looking for a better view. Suddenly, a gloved hand clamps down on his shoulder from behind and roughly spins him around. Lucas finds himself staring at a short man with a hat pulled low over goggled eyes.

The man seizes Lucas hard by both arms and hisses, *"What are you doing here?"*

In a split second, Marco has the man by the throat.

"We're looking for somebody to strangle," he says. "Do you mind?"

"Briggs!" gasps the Gloved Agent. "Anderson!"

Two agents swiftly appear, one at either side of the Gloved Agent. Both look uncertainly at Marco, then at their boss.

"Well?" gags the Gloved Agent. *"Stop him, you morons!"*

Behind them, a loud shriek rises from the crate by the mound.

Marco releases the Gloved Agent. Everyone crouches behind the boxwood shrubs, watching.

Another shriek pierces the night, and I do mean *pierces.* It has a metallic edge to it, like a huge metal fingernail scraping a huge metal blackboard. Imagine chewing a wad of aluminum foil. That's what this shriek feels like.

In the clearing, the beekeepers slowly back away from the crate.

Go Team One

As Cat and Cyril reach Jake, he stares in shock at the roiling water in the lagoon where the two men just disappeared.

"Great . . . silverback . . . apes!" he exclaims.

"Jake," gasps Cyril. "Dude, let's go." He points at the water. "What if it's still hungry?"

"Yeah, let's book, Bixby," says Cat. "This is nuts."

"Okay, okay," says Jake.

As the three kids back away from the water, the bubbles start to move. Jake stops. "It's heading back toward the bridge," he says in a hushed voice.

"Good," says Cyril. "Excellent. Outstanding." He grabs Jake's arm. "Let's go!"

Jake holds up his hand. As the bubbles approach the bridge, the water starts churning more violently. Suddenly a ring of colored lights illuminates under the surface. At first the lights are stationary—red, green, blue, yellow, arrayed in a circle maybe fifteen feet in diameter. Then, slowly, they start to spin.

The water above the lights churns up in a wild, choppy whirlpool.

Jake and Cyril exchange a fierce look.

"That's no creature!" shouts Jake.

"Ring of lights!" screams Cyril. "Where have we seen *that* before?"

"Exactly!"

Powerful vibrations shake the ground under them. The spinning disk of lights now slides beneath the Swilken Burn footbridge. A throbbing, muffled whine rises under the bridge arch.

"What is it?" shouts Cat over the din.

Instinctively, Jake sprints up onto the footbridge. In the middle, he hangs over the stone railing and peers into the depths underneath. The ring of lights is slowly, gradually disappearing.

"It's going down!" he calls out. He can feel the bridge shudder. "It's *diving*."

Cat and Cyril run up onto the bridge behind him.

"Diving where?" says Cat.

Jake gives her a wild, exhilarated look. He points down and says, "See the lights? It's diving into a hole."

Sure enough, the spinning lights reflect off a large round opening.

"Holy Armenian meatballs!" cries Cyril. "That's an underwater tunnel!"

After a few more seconds, the submarine—clearly, that's what it is, kids—slowly banks around a bend in the underwater opening, then zooms out of sight. Only the faint receding glow of its lights can be seen now.

"Cyril!" says Jake. "Do you have your Spy NightWriter flashlight?"

Cyril digs into one of the 472 pockets in his huge cargo pants and whips out a slim flashlight. He tosses it to Jake, who quickly flicks on its blue beam and aims it under the bridge. The light clearly reveals a large underwater hole with a glint of polished metal inside.

"Look!" says Cat, pointing.

A round section of the muddy, algae-covered lagoon floor slowly slides over the hole. Jake watches intently as the camouflaged hatch seals shut. "Where's it going?" he asks. "What does it connect to?" Then it hits him. He turns abruptly to look at Cyril.

"Dude," he says. "Those stories. In the ice-cream shop. And at school."

Cyril's eyes grow wide with awe. He aims two fingers at Jake. "The reservoir!" he says.

"Precisely!" says Jake. He jabs his arm toward the northeast, the direction to the reservoir. "It can't be more than a couple hundred yards from this bridge to the shore of the Lakeside Green."

In a flash, Jake bounds down the bridge and starts sprinting across the fairway.

Cat and Cyril fall in behind him.

"I'll be coughing up my lungs shortly," gasps Cyril, running. His stride is a thing of beauty, resembling a gazelle minus the grace and speed but with a tremendous amount of swaying hair.

"Do you guys do this often?" pants Cat.

"You mean, like, chase submarines that eat people and stuff?" wheezes Cyril. "Yes. Several times per book."

"Impressive," replies Cat.

The trio hits the golf course fence and starts climbing.

⑩

TO THE RESERVOIR

Go Team Two

The Gloved Agent suddenly puts his finger to his ear, where a Spy Link headset rests.

"All units," he whispers tensely. "We have activity at the Hotel. Repeat, activity at the Hotel, over."

Noticing this, Lucas snakes his hand into a pocket, pulls out his own Spy Link headset, and slips it over his ear.

Out in the clearing, the shrieking continues. The crate rattles, and the metallic scraping from inside gets more frantic.

The Gloved Agent swirls around dramatically and glares at his two underlings. "Get these meddling children out of the lockdown area," he hisses quietly. He points warily at Marco. "And take *Kong* here too. Lock them in the mobile unit."

"Yes, sir," whisper the two agents in unison.

The Gloved Agent holds up his gloved hand as he receives a Spy Link message. As he listens, he fails to notice that Lucas is listening as well. "Yes, go ahead, Charlie One," he says briskly.

Nearby, Lucas raises his eyebrows.

You see, what the Gloved Agent has failed to remember is Lucas Bixby's participation in a critical Agency field operation just last February, chronicled in Book 4 of this series, *The Doomsday Dust*. Maybe if the Gloved Agent had read that fine book, he'd have remembered that the Agency's highly secure field frequencies are still coded into Lucas's personal Spy Link receiver unit.

"No, sir," says the Gloved Agent. "I'm not at liberty to speak freely. We have units from, uh, Team Kilo in custody here." His face turns stony and dark. "Well, I guess I fail to see the humor in that, sir, but then . . ." He turns to his agents. "Men, we have another situation developing."

Another loud screech draws all three agents' attention to the crate in the clearing.

Marco and Lexi glance at Lucas, whose eyes are wide with excitement. He leans to them.

"Something's at the reservoir!" he whispers. "It sounds big!"

In the clearing, the beekeepers now stand a good twenty yards from the crate. One of them holds up a slim device—it looks like a TV remote control—and pushes a button.

"Roger, yes sir," continues the Gloved Agent. He rubs his gloved hands together nervously. "They're opening the chamber now. Of course I'll keep you informed. Foxtrot out."

The Gloved Agent turns angrily to Marco and is about to speak when All Holy Heck breaks out in the clearing. The crate's lid flips open. A swarm of black entities bursts out and, shrieking, scrambles up the side of the huge hive. Some look small, like large spiders. Others are bigger, the size of large crabs. All have legs—lots of legs. Wild, wriggling black legs.

Lucas is horrified. He feels faint. Lucas Bixby, as you all know, is deathly afraid of insects.

"Somebody . . . please . . . just throw a blanket over me," he mutters.

Oddly enough, the Gloved Agent and his two minions don't seem particularly surprised by the sight of thousands of creepy, shrieking bugs swarming over a hive the size of a Chevy Tahoe. Lucas correctly guesses that they've seen this sight before. But then something happens that clearly shocks the Agency field team.

The hive erupts.

Yes, with a sickly liquid sound, the top fourth of the earth mound just . . . pops open.

Large, sticky-looking spider-things tumble and hurtle

out of the exposed hole. In the clearing, the four bee-keepers dive behind the forklift truck. One of them howls in fear, but the others are eerily silent.

Behind the boxwoods, the agents spring into action.

"Follow me!" hisses the Gloved Agent. He retreats down the path. Lucas, Lexi, and Marco follow, with the other two agents behind them.

About halfway back to County Road 44, the Gloved Agent suddenly swerves off the path. The kids and Marco follow as he pushes through hostile, clawing branches until he reaches a small, bunkerlike enclosure: an Agency command post.

The Gloved Agent points at a small bench.

"Sit down," he orders.

As Lexi sits, she says, "What were those things?"

"Yeah, Howard," says Marco dryly. "How about an explanation for the tiny children?"

"Stay put, do you hear me?" growls the Gloved Agent, ignoring the questions. "Any attempt to flee will result in the *direst* of consequences." He points an accusing finger at Marco. "Do I make myself clear?"

"Oh, yeah," says Marco with a thin smile.

The Gloved Agent glares at Lucas, who gives him the thumbs-up sign. "You bet!" says Lucas.

Lexi smiles sweetly and nods.

The Gloved Agent turns and rushes off, followed by Agent Briggs and Agent Anderson.

Lucas looks at Lexi, then Marco. "Let's go," he says.

"Right," says Marco.

"Follow me," Lexi says, and dashes through the trees.

As Lucas follows her, he slides off his backpack, opens it, and pulls out two more Spy Link units.

"Time to link up!" he calls.

Go Team One

"Guys, let's link up!" calls Jake Bixby . . . *at the exact same moment!*

Wow. Are these guys brothers, or what?

Jogging across Route 36 to the Lakeside Green, Jake hooks his Spy Link headset over his ear and slides the receiver unit onto his belt. Then he tosses a Spy Link set to Cat; Cyril pulls his own set out of yet another pants pocket. Cat and Cyril "link up" on the run too.

Jake turns on his base unit.

"This is Go Team One, calling Go Team Two, anybody, over?" he calls, panting. "Hello? Anybody?"

Jake! answers Lucas excitedly. **I've been calling you guys!** The excitement in his voice could power a *Nimitz*-class aircraft carrier. **Dude, head for the reservoir, like, now.**

"Dude," says Jake. "We're already there."

What? says Lucas.

Jake quickly tells his brother the Go Team One Story: the men in jumpsuits, the underwater craft "swallowing"

124

them, the tunnel discovery, and the belief that an underground water passage connects the Long Lagoon to the Carrolton Reservoir.

Then, in turn, Lucas recounts the Go Team Two Story: bugging the AMBS truck, the forklift, the trail to the huge hive, the Agency encounter, and the shrieking crate creatures. All of this storytelling is swift and, more importantly, gives the author a chance to sum up the action so far.

"Okay, ten-four on that," says Jake.

"Excellent summary," adds Cyril, glancing at me.

We'll be there shortly, says Lucas. Just listen for a Mazda that sounds like pieces are falling off.

Get out of my car, says Marco's voice.

We're making a left turn, Jake, says Lucas. Expect to arrive in sections.

Get out!

Hey, let go of me! cries Lucas.

Say uncle, replies Marco.

No!

Say uncle!

Aaaaaaa! Let go! Uncle! Uncle!

Jake hears Lexi laughing hysterically. Then, Lucas finally says: I've been humiliated. Over and out.

"Roger that," says Jake. "Out."

The brothers sign off just as Jake, Cat, and Cyril reach the Lakeside Green. The full moon casts an eerie light across the open area. Beyond that, the reservoir looks electrified and alive, like the Long Lagoon did earlier. Jake can picture the two bodies of water connected by an underground vein, sharing energy somehow.

"Somebody's down by the water," says Cat.

Cyril squints. "Where?"

Cat points at a tall, thin figure on the narrow stretch of fresh white sand between the Green and the water. It appears to be a tall man in a ragged-looking gaucho hat. He's carrying a flashlight that he aims down at the water.

Jake takes a few nervous steps, but as he gets closer, he sighs in relief.

"That's Dr. Tim," he says. Then he calls out, "Yo, Dr. Tim!"

The man turns and waves his flashlight.

As they approach him, Jake notices bright flashes of lightning off to his left.

"Is that you, Jake Bixby?" shouts Dr. Tim.

"Yes, Dr. Tim," says Jake. They shake hands. "What's up?"

Now thunder rolls in from the horizon. It's loud.

"Look at that storm moving in," says Dr. Tim, nodding toward a dark tower of moonlit clouds on the western horizon. "I used to study storms. I'm a real scientist, you know."

"Yes, I know," says Jake with a smile.

As the kids turn to look, another jagged spear of lightning illuminates the thunderhead from within. The result is spectacular. Seconds later, another clap of thunder smacks the reservoir.

"Wow," says Cat.

Dr. Tim shakes his head in admiration.

"Looks like a supercell forming," he says, "probably pushing a squall line out front. See the classic anvil-shaped dome on top? The front edge will be here in half an hour, maybe less." As if on cue, a breeze kicks up. "We should get to shelter soon."

"Agreed," says Cyril with a salute. "I'm big on shelter, Dr. Tim. In fact, if I had a million dollars, I'd invest it all in shelter."

Jake indicates the flashlight. "Dr. Tim, are you looking for something in the reservoir?"

"I am, Jake," booms Dr. Tim. He turns and aims his flashlight beam at something in the water.

Cyril leans over and looks. "Whoa, that's sad," he says. "Why would anybody toss a bunch of pumpkins in the reservoir?"

"Those aren't pumpkins," says Dr. Tim.

"What are they?" asks Jake.

"Insect colonies," says Dr. Tim.

"Underwater?"

Dr. Tim nods. "Very strange," he says. He hands the flashlight to Jake, who shines it on the hive cluster. Then Dr. Tim flips open his notebook. "This particular hive configuration has been found in only one other place in the world . . . abandoned, according to these studies," he says, glancing at the pages. "Funny that the species migrated here. Ha! In Carrolton, of all places."

Jake peers down at the hive. "Where else did they find it?" he asks.

"Uzbekistan," says Dr. Tim.

Jake nearly drops the flashlight right into the water. He turns to Dr. Tim, then to Cyril. "Uzbekistan?" repeats Jake.

"Yes, Uzbekistan!" shouts Dr. Tim. "Uzbekistan!"

"Wow, Uzbekistan," says Cyril grimly, nodding his hair. The guys all look at Cat. She smiles.

"Uzbekistan," she says.

Cyril claps her on the shoulder. "Well done," he says. "Thanks."

Dr. Tim holds up his notebook to display a page with a map. Jake lights it with the flashlight. It's a map of, hmmm, let's see . . . hey, it's Uzbekistan!

"What *part* of Uzbekistan?" asks Jake.

Dr. Tim jabs his finger at the map. "This part," he says. As he points, another bright yellow bolt lights up the clouds to the west. Seconds later, thunder shudders across the sky.

At the same moment, Cat's cell phone rings.

She answers. "Hi, Mom," she says. "S'up?"

While she listens to the reply, Dr. Tim points again to a blue spot on the map. It's labeled CHARVAK RESERVOIR . . . located, as the map clearly shows, not far from the cratered Kyrk-Tau region south of Samarkand, the area described by both Marco and the Dark Man clear back in Chapter 6, an award-winning chapter if ever there was one.

"That's the place, all right," says Jake, exchanging a glance with Cyril.

"Yeah, I figured," says Cat into her phone. "I'm just down the street. See you in about ninety seconds. Yes, love you too." She clacks the phone shut, sighs, and looks at Cyril. "Gotta go."

"Home?" asks Cyril.

"Yep," says Cat. "Mom hates storms."

"Should I walk you?" asks Cyril.

"Walk me? Why? Am I a dog?"

Cyril clears his throat. "Do you really want me to answer that?" he says.

Cat punches his shoulder. "I live four blocks from here. I can manage. And, anyway, you should get home too."

"I agree," says Cyril. He looks out at the black water.

Cat gives Cyril a quick hug. "Thanks, buster," she says. "Gosh, you really know how to show a girl a good time."

"Heh," says Cyril, glowing bright red and then exploding. The Pieces of Cyril crawl back together and re-form Cyril, except backward.

Cat runs off across the green.

Jake grins at Cyril. "Sweet," he says.

"Shut up."

"The girl's right, we should go," says Dr. Tim, gazing at the cloud wall to the west.

A small jet of water suddenly splashes up from the reservoir, not far from the shore. Then another one. And another.

"Why are the fish jumping?" asks Cyril.

Dr. Tim grabs the flashlight and shines it down at the colony complex. Black, insectlike creatures are pouring out of the hives. Some are small and antlike. But a few are huge, by insect standards—more like small crabs or lobsters.

Some of them shoot to the surface, wriggle into the air, and fall back in.

Jake, Cyril, and Dr. Tim start backing away from the shore.

Suddenly, a violent wind kicks up. The gusts are so strong, they blow off Dr. Tim's gaucho hat and whip Cyril's hair into a frenzy.

Jake stares off to the west. "How'd the storm get here so fast?" he shouts over the wind.

Dr. Tim looks around in confusion. "This isn't weather!" he shouts.

Then they hear a low, whispery thrumming in the sky. The three look up to see a pair of huge, black, insect-shaped stealth helicopters hovering almost directly above them.

"The Agency!" screams Cyril.

Now an urgent, amplified voice calls down from above.

"Clear the area *immediately!*" The loudspeaker crackles and pops. "You are in extreme danger. I repeat, *clear the area!*"

The water near the shore is torn into spray by rotor wind . . . and it boils with black, flailing legs.

11

THUNDER ON THE WATER

Marco's silver Mazda screeches into the Lakeside Green parking lot just as a dazzling, green-tinted spotlight bursts from the sky and hits the reservoir. Lucas hops out of the car and sprints toward three pale ghosts by the water, with Lexi and Marco right on his tail.

Two of the ghosts are running in his direction. Hey, it's Jake and Cyril!

"What the monkey is happening?" shouts Lucas as he nears them. "And who's that?" he adds, looking toward the shore.

As the two teams meet up, Jake and Cyril spin to look back.

"Hey, Dr. Tim isn't following us," says Jake, trying to shade his eyes from the spot's harsh glare. He watches the gaunt figure lean out over the water. "What's he doing?"

"Those crablike crab things are going berserk," gasps Cyril. "They'll eat him alive!"

"Crab things?" says Marco.

"In the water," Jake says, nodding briskly. "Coming out of hives, left and right."

"It's crabbish madness, I tell you," says Cyril.

"I don't like this," says Marco.

"Why isn't Dr. Tim running away too?" asks Lucas.

Up above, the helicopters hover lower, and the loud-speaker repeats its warning. Another spotlight from the second helicopter hits the surface. Between the copter blades and the swarming underwater legs, the green-lit reservoir looks like white-water rapids in a mountain stream.

But Dr. Tim ignores all the tumult. Crouching, he calmly dips his hand into the water.

The Bixby brothers look unbelieving at each other for a brief second. Then:

"Let's go!" shouts Jake.

Now kids, "Let's go!" can mean a *lot* of different things. For example, it can mean: "Let's get out of here before the hive creatures crack open our heads and eat our brains!" But these Bixbys, well . . . you know what "Let's go!" means to a Bixby.

Jake and Luke run directly toward the water.

"What are you doing, Dr. Tim?" calls Jake as he approaches the scientist.

"Crabbing," shouts Dr. Tim over the whine of chopper blades. With a grizzly grin, he pulls his hand from the water clutching a large, black, eight-legged . . . uh, crab thing.

He holds the beast up by one leg as it wriggles wildly.

"*Aaaaaagghh!*" scream Jake and Lucas, backing away from it.

"Relax," shouts Dr. Tim. He shines his flashlight on the creature. Its slick black body seems to absorb the light. "See? No chelae."

"Chelae?" asks Jake.

"Claws," explains Dr. Tim. He examines the creature, holding it up higher. "No pincers, either. And barely a mouth, with nothing that can be described as teeth or chewing mouthparts." He nods sagely. "I've been studying these things all week."

As he speaks, Lexi and Marco arrive.

"Ugh!" says Lexi, making a face.

Even Marco looks a little queasy at the sight of the squirming organism. "Wow," he says. "That's disgusting."

"*Evacuate the reservoir area immediately!*" screams the loudspeaker from above.

As everyone looks upward, another jagged trident of lightning splits open the sky. For a brief second the sleek, insect-shaped helicopters are clearly visible against the illuminated backdrop. Then everything goes black again, and a sharp crack of thunder follows just seconds later.

Marco says, "Say, maybe we should, like, get out of here."

Dr. Tim gives a dismissive wave at the helicopters.

"They're idiots!" he bellows. "There's no danger here." He glares angrily at Marco. "I told them that yesterday."

"Yesterday?" says Marco, clearly surprised.

"Yes!" shouts Dr. Tim. "Yesterday morning I reported my initial findings to the National Science Institute. Two hours later, those fools appeared at my door"—he points at the helicopters—"asking some of the most gibbering, dimwitted questions I've ever heard." He glowers up at the sky. "Especially the one with the gloves. The man is a—"

His sentence is cut off by the loudspeaker again.

"This is your final warning!" crackles the voice from above.

Everyone stares up into the spotlight.

The voice blares: "You are impeding a national security operation of the United States government. So . . . get out!" There is a pause as forking lightning rips through the cloud wall to the west. Then: "We're not kidding!"

"Yes," says Marco, smiling at Dr. Tim. "You're right on the money there, pal. But I was referring to that storm. It looks big."

"Oh, right," says Dr. Tim. "Yes, let's go. It's not safe."

As if to confirm this statement, screeching tires signal the arrival of several black Agency cars in the parking lot. Doors fly open, and men burst out wearing dark suits and night-vision goggles just as another earsplitting cannonade of thunder rolls across the reservoir from the west.

And then it happens.

Out in the deep water, maybe a hundred yards from shore, a loud shriek pierces through the hubbub. A large jet of white water shoots straight up into the darkening sky. Several huge black appendages thrust up through the surface.

Lexi points at it.

"The Black Hand!" she gasps.

The entity rises vertically from the water like a leaping whale and falls forward, slapping the surface with a mighty splash. White spray explodes in all directions. Then the creature, its humped back visible, glides toward the shore.

"It's coming right at us!" shouts Cyril.

Everyone scrambles away. Everyone, that is, except Dr. Tim.

"Get back, Dr. Tim!" shouts Lexi in alarm.

Dr. Tim looks back at Lexi and the others. But he doesn't move.

A squad of agents hurries down from the parking lot

toward Team Spy Gear. One of them barks into a Spy Link headset. "Charlie Two, we have Bogey Bravo approaching!" he shouts. "Repeat, bogey to shore, bogey to shore! Code Bravo! Clear the area! Clear the area!"

As the monster approaches the beach, the gradual ramp of sand forces it farther up out of the water. Green spotlights hit it, revealing something that resembles a massive jet-black starfish. Four flipperlike arms, two on each side, stroke gracefully, pushing its large, thick body through the water. A fifth appendage juts forward, like a head. But this "head" has nothing resembling a face or eyes or mouth. In fact, it has no features whatsoever. It looks like a fifth arm.

"Holy tank traps!" exclaims Lucas, both horrified and fascinated at the same time.

The Black Hand scuttles through shallow water, now nearly ashore. It heads straight for Dr. Tim, who continues to stand unmoving, like a statue.

"It's going to eat him!" screams Lexi.

"Run, Dr. Tim, run!"

"Establish a control perimeter!" shouts one agent as the others fan out across the beach. "Lockdown! Move! Move! Move!"

"Get out of there, Dr. Tim!"

"Dr. Tim! Dr. Tim!"

The black helicopters hover lower.

More chain-lightning zigzags and thunder detonates at nearly the same moment. It seems like the whole world is shuddering.

The storm is at hand!

But Dr. Tim calmly watches the approaching beast. Its blackness is like a living shadow, so perfect that it seems to absorb the green spotlights, neutralizing them, turning light into dark. Dr. Tim does not flinch, not even when The Black Hand shrieks hideously and rears up directly in front of him. As it flails its arms, a web of lightning shocks the sky behind it like, like . . . *like a bad horror film!* Thunder pounds the ground, drowning out the monster's harsh, horrific screams.

Then The Black Hand lurches forward.

It falls nearly on top of Dr. Tim, but lands just short.

It hits the sand with a wet splat.

And it disintegrates with a buzzing hiss.

That's right: disintegrates.

Each black appendage, including the head, breaks apart into a writhing mass of black insects.

Whew!

That's so freaky that I need another space break before I go on.

The swarms scamper up the beach with a soft hiss. As the five bug columns scramble past him in different directions,

Dr. Tim watches calmly. Then, with a big grin, he turns to the kids and Marco.

"Awesome!" he says.

Stunned, Jake takes a step forward. One swarm moves toward him but splits into two columns as it gets closer, each one bending in an arc around him, then rejoining on the other side.

"That's . . . incredible," says Jake, looking down at the streaming bugs.

"It's an amphibious super-organism!" shouts Dr. Tim. "The perfect life-form for a water planet like Earth."

Marco suddenly hops over one of the insect columns and grabs Jake's shoulder. "We're getting out of here right now, Bixby," he says. "That's a violent storm approaching, and there's nothing else we can do here." He gestures toward the Agency field team, who look confused and unsettled by the bizarre transformation of The Black Hand into orderly columns of seemingly harmless insects. "Let them clean up here," concludes Marco. "I'm taking you home."

Jake nods. He hears the concern in Marco's voice. He says, "Okay."

But when Jake turns to the other kids, he sees Lucas fiddling with a Spy Link base unit hooked to his belt. The younger Bixby's eyes are wide with excitement.

"What is it?" calls Jake.

"I'm patched into the Agency field channel," replies

Lucas. He looks up at Marco. "Something else is happening."

"Where?" Marco asks.

Lucas turns to the water. "Out there," he says.

A new burst of activity suddenly rolls across the beach like a wave. Shadows are running to and fro, and both helicopters suddenly bank hard and zoom out toward the center of the reservoir.

And then everyone sees it. In the water.

The rippling disk of colored lights, circling in the depths. Then rising.

Then a dark oval bursts through the surface like the explosion of a depth charge. Wow! The droning craft rises into the air, its lights spinning. Its ascension seems almost painfully slow as the green spotlights hit it and the helicopters close in.

We've all seen that craft before, eh, Spy Gear fans?

"Viper!" shouts Cyril.

For a brief moment the airship hovers and seems unable to rise farther.

"Something's wrong with him!" shouts Lucas, waving his arms. "Get him now! *Get him!*"

And indeed the helicopters are so close, it seems any agent could leap across, rip open a hatch, and pull Viper out by the scruff of his neck. But then the airship begins to tilt ever so slightly. It starts edging toward the opposite shore of the reservoir. And then a towering jet of water shoots like a geyser from the fuselage. The engines whine loudly.

"It's clearing its tanks or something!" exclaims Cyril.

Now the craft picks up speed, arcing upward, with the black helicopters in hot pursuit.

Lucas, listening to his Spy Link, suddenly jumps up and down. "Dudes, they've scrambled two F-16s from Waxman Air Force Base," he gasps in awe. "Ha! He won't get away *this* time!"

As the flicker of airborne colored lights moves off to the north, the front edge of the thunderstorm begins to shake the tree line just a few hundred meters to the southwest.

And then, high in the sky to the north, a brilliant white flash illuminates everything like a midnight sun for several seconds.

A booming concussion rolls across the reservoir.

Was that thunder? Or something else?

"They got him, right?" shouts Cyril. He looks wildly over at Jake. "Did they get him?"

"I don't know," says Jake, blinking away the image of the blast.

"Let's go!" shouts Marco. "The storm is here!"

(12)

GEAR'S END?

Team Spy Gear is sitting in Marco's car when the first big raindrops hit. Jake is speaking via cell phone to Mrs. Bixby, assuring her that everyone's safe and will be home in minutes.

As he hangs up in record short time, he sees a huge, caped silhouette floating toward the car. It is, of course, the Dark Man.

Cyril, who sits in the front passenger seat, cranks down his window. "Darth!" he shouts. "Over here!"

The Dark Man steps to Cyril's window. He leans down.

From the backseat, Lucas calls, "We heard your field reports. Wow!"

"Yes, I know," says the Dark Man wearily. "And that's why I must ask now for your field units."

Lucas looks aghast. "Our Spy Links?" he blurts.

"Correct."

Everyone in the car hands over their Spy Link units to Marco, who slips them into a bag.

"Time to let the adults handle things," says Marco.

"What?" says Lucas.

"Yes, Briggs!" barks the Dark Man.

Lucas is confused, but then sees that the Dark Man is now speaking into his own Spy Link headset.

"Yes, shut it down," orders the Dark Man. Then he turns to Jake. "Mr. Bixby, please be advised that Stoneship Woods is now a fully restricted area. The community will be told of a mosquito infestation. West Nile virus, I think. But, Mr. Bixby, you of course will know the truth. We have a delicate extermination to perform, and we must fully dismantle our facility as well."

"The warehouse," says Jake.

"Yes, the warehouse," says the Dark Man.

"You're tearing it apart."

"Something we should have done long ago," says the Dark Man. He turns to Lucas. "And we'll need your gear, please."

Lucas looks stunned. Numbly, he hands his gadget backpack to the Dark Man.

The Dark Man seizes it and turns to Marco.

"You're right," he says. "It has been a reckless mistake to involve these children, and I apologize." He looks back at Lucas. His voice softens behind the filter mask. "Please do not misunderstand, young man. Your participation has been . . . valuable, certainly. But it is now officially terminated."

Lucas leans forward from the backseat. He stares at the back of Marco's head.

"We were a mistake?" he says.

Marco twists to face Lucas. His teeth are set. "Yes," he says.

The intensity with which he says this makes Lucas sit back in his seat.

Jake reaches over and clasps his brother's shoulder.

"Let's go home, dude," he says.

In the distance, men are shouting. Rain spatters on the Dark Man's hat as he abruptly pulls away from the Mazda's window to attend to his grim business.

Cyril rolls up the window to keep the rain out.

Marco jams the gearstick forward. *Clank!*

As the car pulls away, Jake presses his face against the window to look back toward the lakefront beach. Huge, dark figures are moving here and there, with great purpose. One of the helicopters is making a beach landing. Jake catches a glimpse of four big agents escorting Dr. Tim toward the dark, willowy craft that rocks in the great gusts of wind.

Then everything melts together behind thick sheets of rain.

• • •

Back in the Bixby brothers' bedroom, four wet kids slump in various attitudes of defeat. They look like melting statues, actually.

Jake sits backward on his desk chair. His baseball cap is wet. His shoes are wet. Man, *everything* is wet. It's raining so hard, he got completely soaked just running from Marco's car to the front porch.

Jake stares down at the carpet. That's not like Jake Bixby.

After a minute or so of silence, he looks around the room.

"Well, *that* was fun," he says.

Rain pounds like drums on Carrolton. It hasn't rained like this in years. Nearby, Cyril sits on Jake's bed. He stares at the Bixby's computer screen. The computer isn't on.

Cyril says, "Gee, I'm glad we didn't ruin anything." He looks over at Jake. "Since we were in everybody's way, being that we're just, you know, little kids and such." He shakes his wet hair, which creates a small monsoon in the room. Trees fall over. He adds, "Pretty much we're like stupid but adorable puppies, apparently, or whatever."

Lexi lies on her back on the floor near the computer desk. She's nearly hidden by a pile of books, clothes, old food, and broken science projects that have things sticking out of them. She tosses a tennis ball straight up in the air, then catches it, over and over.

Finally, she says, "Why do you have a tennis ball?"

Lucas says, "Frankly, I don't know."

"Do you play tennis?" she asks.

Lucas just looks at her.

"Okay," she says. She pushes herself up to her elbows and sighs. "I guess I just wondered why you have a tennis ball."

"Because he's a kid," says Cyril. "Kids have tennis balls for no apparent reason. We find them in odd places . . . like, in the woods, next to trees with eyes. And then we bring them home." He lies back on the bed. "And then bad guys conquer the world."

Jake looks over at Cyril.

"The Agency is probably tracking Viper down right now," he says.

"Oh, well, *that* makes me feel better," says Cyril. He puts his hands behind his head. "Now I can retire. Hang up the old gumshoes."

"Yeah," says Lucas. "The Agency has such a good history of really *closing in for the kill* when they've got Viper in their sites."

Jake grins a little. Staring at the ceiling, he says, "Well, in any case, there's nothing we can do about it, because—"

"Because we're just little kids," interrupts Cyril.

"Exactly," says Jake. "So we should stay out of their way. And go play." He nods. "With trucks."

"And, like, action figures," agrees Cyril.

"Right."

"Fun!"

"Let's do it!"

Suddenly, Lexi's cell phone rings. She digs it out of her pocket and looks at the incoming number. "It's my cousin," she says.

"Cousin?" repeats Cyril.

Lexi flips the phone open and says, "Hey, Marco."

"Oh, you mean *Mr. Backstabber*," says Cyril darkly.

Lexi listens for a few seconds, then starts nodding. She says, "Okay, I'll tell them. Bye." She hangs up.

"Tell them what?" says Lucas.

"He says he's sorry," says Lexi.

Lucas stares at her. "That's it?" he says.

Lexi nods. "And he said the bugs are dark."

"Dark?"

"Yeah, dark," says Lexi. She looks around at the guys.

"You mean, like, genetically engineered dark matter bugs?" asks Lucas.

Lexi shrugs. "He said: 'The bugs are dark.' Then he said to tell everyone he's sorry about what happened, and he'll be gone a few weeks."

"Gee," says Cyril, stretching his arms and clamping them behind his head. "I'll bet Uzbekistan is *lovely* this time of year."

"Why does *he* get to go spy and we don't?" whines Lucas. "That's not fair."

"Marco doesn't have any math homework, son," explains Cyril patiently. "So you see, he has more time to *save the world* than we do."

Now everybody sits in silence. *Subdued* silence, which of course is the worst kind.

Finally, Jake stands up.

"Okay," he says. "This is ridiculous."

Lucas looks up at his big brother. "What is?" he asks.

Jake says, "We can't just sit around feeling sorry for ourselves."

"Why not?" asks Cyril.

Jake grabs a handful of Cyril's hair and gives a gentle tug. "Because," he says.

"Ouch," says Cyril. "That hurts, but I like your logic."

"Look, there's something in Stoneship Woods," says Jake. "Those are *our* woods. Nobody knows them better than we do." He lets go of Cyril's hair. "We need to find out what's going on."

"But Dark Man said to stay away," says Lexi.

Jake says, "So?"

Lexi sits up. "He's the boss."

"Says who?"

This silences everyone for a second. Four minds start cranking loudly. It's deafening, I tell you. I can hear it from clear up here in the space station.

"Okay, dudes," says Jake finally. "These adults, they think they know everything. Maybe they do. But it seems to me that they . . . don't."

Cyril nods. "You've got a point there."

"So listen up," begins Jake.

Okay, so everybody's listening. Even me.

First, Jake looks at Lucas. He says, "Do you believe the Omega Link?"

Lucas frowns. "What do you mean?" he asks.

"I mean, like, its last message," says Jake.

"You mean the plea for help?"

"Yes," says Jake. "That. Do you believe it? Do you think it's a true message?"

Lucas thinks for a moment. "Actually," he says, "I do."

"Somebody, somewhere, is calling us for help?" asks Jake.

"Yes," says Lucas. "Yes."

"And not just calling *anyone*," says Jake. "Not calling the Agency. Not the Dark Man. No, somebody is calling *us* for help." He jabs a thumb at his chest. "*Us*. The plea was to the Bixbys, right?"

Lucas nods slowly.

Jake turns to both Cyril and Lexi. "And if they're calling us, well, then they're calling *you* guys too."

"Yes, of course," says Cyril. "Everybody knows we're practically Bixbys."

"So what should we do about it?" asks Jake.

Cyril raises his hand.

"Yes, Cyril?" says Jake, pointing to him.

Cyril stands up.

"Give up," he says, "and cry like babies."

He takes a bow and sits down.

"Yes, that's an option," says Jake. "We can quit. We can decide that adults will take care of things." He looks at Lexi. "The Agency. The Dark Man. Even Marco. We can just let *them* handle it." He turns back to Cyril, his best friend for life. "We can go to school every day," says Jake, "then come home and play with trucks."

"Normally, that would sound good to me," says Cyril.

"But what about now?" asks Jake.

A blast of thunder rattles the window. They all look at it. Then Cyril squints. He clacks his teeth together a few times, thinking.

"Well, now I'm *conflicted*," he says.

"Let's take a team vote," says Jake. "Should we quit this case and just return to being little kids, like we're supposed to?"

"Yes," says Cyril. Then he looks around at everybody's eyes. "Okay, no."

"Good answer," says Jake with a grin.

"Somebody needs our help," says Lucas. "That's the bottom line."

Jake nods. The brothers slap hands and pound fists.

Cyril rubs his hair. "And, hey, I figure if I don't get to

the bottom of what 'Flush the mantis' means, I'll probably go insane and start talking to chickens," he says. "So I have selfish motives."

"I want to catch Viper," says Lexi.

Cyril spins and glares at her. "Did anybody *ask* your opinion?"

"No," says Lexi happily.

Cyril smacks his hands together. "*I didn't think so,*" he yells. "Now let's get to work."

Lucas is bouncing on his bed: *Boiing! Boiing!* Jake and Cyril do their secret Assyrian handshake. Lexi punches the computer's power button. Soon everyone is gathered around Cyril, who sits at the keyboard tapping away like the mad fiend that he is. One thing about the Internet, kids: It does, in fact, give you power. Oh sure, it's full of bad guys, too. But so is the *real* world. You just have to deal with it. Sorry, but that's the way it is. That's why we have spies.

And, suddenly, *whooooosh!* The spycam view backs out of the Bixby bedroom window.

Yeah, I hear you, readers:

Whoa! Wait! We can't leave yet!

But, trust me: Team Spy Gear really needs some privacy right now.

They have a *lot* of work to do.

Here's why: Viper's on the prowl. Yes, those big

Agency grown-ups missed him. Amazing! He slipped away, right through their fingers, right through the storm clouds.

So back, back we go, back up into the sky for The Big Satellite Picture.

Hmmm. From way up here, things look pretty dang dark.

But, hey, check out over there! There, in Uzbekistan!

Did you guys see that weird flash of light?

AUTHOR ACKNOWLEDGMENTS

Time to thank two special folks who make Spy Gear work a joy.

First, to Ralph Giuffre ("Ralph the Mighty"), for suggesting the idea of telling Spy Gear stories in the first place, and then for being as good a business partner and friend as a guy could have.

Second, thanks to my editor, Jennifer Klonsky (beware the "Klonsky Toll Road"), who fires and then rehires me regularly. Her guidance and wit have kept me on track and, frankly, scared to death. But in a good way.

Here's a sneak peek at . . .

ADVENTURES

THE OMEGA OPERATIVE

Hey, something's going on down there.

It looks suspicious.

Check out that small convoy of Russian-made KamAZ-535 military transport trucks. See it?

No, not the one in Tajikistan. You've panned too far east again. You guys are always panning too far east. Come on, people! Let's get those KH-12 spy satellites under control. Those trucks in Tajikistan are just practicing for their impending invasion of England. We don't care about that. Pan *west!*

There, *that* convoy: The one rumbling up the high pass in the eastern mountains of Uzbekistan.

The road is very dry, so the big Russian trucks kick

up a lot of dust.[1] Dust is everywhere. I can't see clearly, even though my spy telescope is so incredibly powerful. I need a better viewing angle. I'd really like to pilot the International Space Station just a little bit to the left, but that's hard to do when you're hiding in a closet.[2]

So you're asking, *What's so suspicious about a bunch of trucks driving through a mountain pass in Uzbekistan?* To that, I would answer, *Nothing . . . at first glance.* And so you'd take a second glance, maybe even a third, and then say, *You know, Rick, I still don't see anything particularly suspicious.* At that point I would accidentally hit the off button to cut radio transmission.

Wait. There it is.

The trucks are stopping. Two men jump out of the cab in the lead vehicle.

They walk up to a solid granite rock face rising up on the left side of the road. As they approach, a section of the rock tilts upward, revealing a cave opening large enough for, say, a convoy of trucks to enter, one by one. The two men return to the lead vehicle, and the convoy of trucks enters, one by one.

As the last truck enters the side of the cliff wall, it

---

1. Big Russian trucks are designed to kick up a lot of dust even when it isn't dusty. Kids, this is the kind of secret fact you learn from watching movies *very carefully*.

2. If the astronauts find me, they'll beat me up . . . which might be kind of fun in zero gravity, now that I think of it. Or else they'll just make me do all the cleaning, which would *suck*.

grinds to a sudden halt. We see the rear flap of the truck flutter a bit.

Now the driver appears. He walks around to the rear of the truck and crouches to examine something under the rear gate.

Then, suddenly, something thrusts through the flap.

It looks like a pair of giant claws—the claws of, say, a praying mantis.

Quick as lightning, these claws snatch the man into the back of the big Russian truck.

Okay, now . . . *that* was creepy.

We'd better go report this to the Bixbys, eh, fellow spies?

First, swivel left. Stick your arms straight up like Superman and then rocket at Mach 17 around the gentle blue curve of the planet.[3] When you see North America, pitch downward and re-enter the atmosphere so you can breathe again, unless you're already dead, in which case you'll just have to keep orbiting. As you descend, the air pressure really builds, so try not to implode. Nobody wants to see extruded human jelly tumbling through the air, especially during meals.

Okay, you're doing really well.

---

3. If your face starts to melt, you might want to slow down a bit.

Now aim for the middle of the continent.

Wow, it's summertime there. Very hot and humid. Very unpleasant. Really, if Iberian monkeys hadn't invented air conditioning during the last ice age, I think we'd all be in trouble, especially because of the monkey smell.

Aha! Look down there. That's Carrolton, where the Bixby brothers live.

Keep diving. It's getting hotter, isn't it?

That's because summer in Carrolton was invented by guys who planned to use the entire city to bake bread. But then people moved in, homesteaders and whatnot. This of course was back in the 1400s, when people were stupid and only had one arm. Kids, I highly recommend that you read history books about those early days of our nation. You'll laugh so hard!

Anyway, as you tumble screaming toward Carrolton, veer toward the north end of town.

Look! It's Cyril Wong. He's walking with Lexi Lopex. Two other kids, both strangers, troop along beside them. These two strangers look and act like brothers, but they can't be, because it's Tuesday. On Tuesday, of course, nobody is brothers. Or wait. Maybe I'm thinking of Carrolton's Tuesday ban on downtown parking, which is different from "being brothers." So maybe those two boys *are* brothers. Maybe not. There's only one sure way to find out.

As you slam into the ground next to them at 600 mph, notice how they talk to each other.

Let's listen in, shall we?

Tromping along, Cyril glances around at the surrounding neighborhood lawns.

Why are all these people slamming into the ground from outer space? he wonders to himself. But he says nothing about it. Instead, he turns to one of the two strangers, the older one, and says, "Jake, I've been thinking."

"Uh-oh," answers the tall strange boy.

"No, don't worry, dude, this time it has nothing to do with hair or hair-related issues or hair products," Cyril reassures him.

The smaller of the two strange boys gives his possible big brother a look.

"It has something to do with Stoneship Woods, I'll wager," says the small strange boy. "Or my name isn't Lucas Bixby."

Strong statement. But who are these strange boys? Maybe we can get a clue from Lexi, who whips forward into a few quick cartwheels as she moves along.

"I think . . . it's time . . . we went . . . back in," she says, cartwheeling.

Cyril stares over at her. "Is that right?" he says.

"Yes," says Lexi.

"Why?"

"Because it's time," she replies.

Cyril nods. "I see your logic there," he says with a thoughtful rub of his chin.

Lexi does a couple of spin moves, then bows. She's in a great mood today. "I think we should all go into the woods, climb some trees, and spy," she says with a bright smile. "And I should be leader."

Cyril looks at the two strangers. "Well, Bixbys, what say ye to that?"

"Hear, hear," says the taller unknown character with a killer grin. "Agreed, Lucas?"

"I'm all for it, Jake," says the smaller fellow whose name and identity nobody can figure out. "I think Team Spy Gear has given the Agency plenty of time to solve things on their own." He nods at Lexi. "Guys, you can only give adults so much time before you should step in and clean up their mess."

Okay, well, let's move on, shall we?

We really need to find the Bixbys, or else we'll just have to stop the book right here.

Here's another sneak peek, this time from the first book in the OUTRIDERS series by Ed Decter:

#1 EXPEDITION TO BLUE KEY

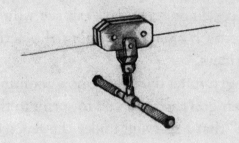

Getting hit by a golf ball hurts. Really hurts. It's bad enough when it happens by accident, but I had two angry golfer dudes *aiming* golf balls at me. I don't know the rules of golf, but I discovered that golfers get really furious if you pick up the ball they are playing with and stuff it in your backpack. That's why I was running.

I had been farming golf balls in the woods near the Bluffs Country Club. For some reason, the members of the Bluffs Club never called the trees and bushes around the golf course "the woods." They called it "the rough." But whatever it was called, there were thousands of hardly used golf balls just waiting to be harvested. Each golf ball (if it hadn't been smashed up too much) was worth twenty-five cents to Chuck at Surf Island Discount Golf and Tennis. Expeditions need supplies and supplies cost money. So you can see why golf ball farming was *critical* for funding the activities of the Outriders.

The angry golfer dudes were now zooming toward me in their golf cart, so I had to sprint to the "guest entrance" that I had dug under the fence that surrounded the golf course. My backpack was so fat with harvested balls, it took some work to yank it under the chain link fence. Once I was on the other side, though, I knew I was safe. The angry golfers were too big to make it through the guest entrance, and no way were they going to try to make it *over* the fence because of the barbed wire. To get to the Escape Trail, I had to scramble over the edge of the bluff and drop down onto this hidden ledge of rock that overlooks my hometown of Surf Island.

Surf Island is divided into two parts:

PART ONE: The hilly part (where I was standing) is called the Bluffs, where you find:

1. People with really big houses
2. New model cars that go with the houses
3. The Bluffs Country Club, where we farm balls and gain access to a bunch of electric golf carts that can be started without a key (if you know how)

PART TWO: The flat part, which is called the Flats, where you find:

1. People with really small houses
2. Old-model cars that go with the houses
3. The Sternmetz Marina (named for some naval dude Commodore Sternmetz, who died at sea or something). The marina always smelled like decaying fish guts, and if you grew up inside the "circle of aroma," that's how you knew you were really from the Flats.

My immediate problem was that the Flats was about two hundred feet below my current position. The only way to get down there was on the Escape Trail, but it is steep—way too steep to carry the backpack full of golf balls, so that's why we installed the zip line.

In one of the rusty piles of boat junk at his dad's salvage yard at the marina, my friend Wyatt found an old winch cable (more on Wyatt and his dad later). The cable must have been used to tow buoys or something because it was really thick and extra-long, which was exactly what we needed to make the zip line.

We attached one end of the winch cable to this pine tree that jutted out from the hidden ledge (where I was standing) and dropped the other end all the way down to the Good Climbing Tree in my best friend Shelby's backyard (more on her later—be patient). At the end of a normal golf ball farming expedition I would hook my backpack onto this thing called a trolley pulley and let the pack fly down through the trees (all those branches hid the cable really well), and then, when I got down to the bottom of the trail, I could climb up the tree in Shelby's yard and retrieve the balls. But this wasn't going to be a normal day.

Apparently those golfer dudes were *hugely* ticked off and had found some way through the chain-link fence (maybe through one of the groundskeeper's gates), and I could hear them crunching through the bushes right above me. All they had to do was peer over the edge of the bluff and they would have spotted me on the ledge. Not only would I be toast, but the golfers might discover the zip line, and that would be *really* serious because it would choke off a major source of funds for our expeditions and get me and Wyatt in ultra-bad trouble for scavenging the winch cable in the first place. At this point I had two options:

Option 1: Get caught.
Option 2: Toss the backpack and disappear down the Escape Trail.

I did not like either option so I chose:

Option 3: Hook my backpack to the trolley pulley and RIDE WITH IT down the zip line.

It was a good thing that the winch cable was so strong, but kind of a bad thing that the backpack's straps weren't—I fell about thirty feet straight down into a thick clump of some kind of dark green crawling vine. This viny stuff (I don't know much about plants) broke my fall, so I didn't fracture any bones or anything. I just had to pray that it wasn't poison ivy.

I had fallen in an area of the Bluffs we had never

explored before, which was unusual because my friends and I had been all over these hills. There was a local rumor that before the Revolutionary War some pirate had stashed doubloons or jewels or something in these hills. In fact, that naval guy Commodore Sternmetz was lost at sea while he was hunting down the pirate. None of us in the Outriders believed there really was a chest of British treasure hidden up here, but the idea kind of lived in the back of our minds, so while we were blazing trails or "scavenging" stuff we kept our eyes open—you know, just in case. I carried my now-strapless backpack (seemed *much* heavier) and pushed my way past the mossy rocks and through the thick undergrowth toward Shelby's backyard, where we had hidden an old barrel that we called the Ball Barrel, where we siloed our farmed golf balls.

Shelby (my best friend, remember?) is actually the most important *person* in this story, but I need to tell you about one last *place* before I can get back to her.

BLUE CAVE

Blue Cave got its name because (and this was explained to us by Mr. Mora) every seven years this really weird kind of plankton drifts into the cave and starts to GLOW. Mr. Mora calls it "bioluminescent," which is a fancy way of saying it glows in the dark and lights up the cave with blue light. This only happens for, like, a couple of days in July. I don't know why it happens only in July. (I don't know much about plankton.)

But the important thing to remember is that this blue glow thing only happens ONCE EVERY SEVEN YEARS, which means I was five the last time that it happened. The next time it starts to glow I'll be nineteen (I'm twelve now, if you're math challenged), and when I'm nineteen I'll probably be away in Fiji on the pro surf tour, so that's why we knew we had to get out there *in the next few days* and not any other time. We had to assemble the Outriders and *get moving* or we would miss it all. Maybe forever.

The thing about Blue Cave is that it's about twelve miles away from Surf Island, which wouldn't be much of a problem if you could get there in an older sister's car or on a bike, but you can't. The only way to get there is by sea, so you need a boat or a kayak or a para-surfboard, all of which we had "access" to, but of course none of us "owned" ourselves. (I'll explain the rules and regulations about why "scavenging" and "stealing" are two different things at another time.) Put it this way: It was *possible* to make it all the way to Blue Cave, but there were two tremendous problems.

TREMENDOUS PROBLEM NUMBER 1

Shelby has these parents who kind of think she's better than everyone else (might be true). Her parents also aren't exactly thrilled about her choice of friends (mostly me). Shelby's really awesome at school stuff. She's like a super-brain. In some ways she's Little Miss Perfect, but she doesn't raise her hand and wave it all frantic when she knows the answer to something (which she always does). She is really into gymnastics, which makes her kind of tensed out, because if you fall just once your whole competition is ruined, which is why I like surfing, 'cause you can wipe out and still come back and charge the next wave. Anyway, her parents kind of expect a lot from her—they "set the bar high" and want her to leave Surf Island and go to a good college. They don't have loads of bucks, so they want Shelby to "excel" in academics and that's why they stuck her in summer school, so she could get "ahead credits." It is hard to believe there are parents roaming around on this earth who would be so cruel as to make a super-smart kid go to summer school. Sure, if you flunk everything left and right, you could make a case for summer school, but not for Shelby. She could *teach* summer school! But her parents' twisted logic was that if she got ahead credits she could take even more advanced classes in high school and get some kind of scholarship for college. They keep telling Shelby (and at one time me, but they've given up) that every class and every test she takes is "connected" like the "links of a chain" (these are their words, not mine).

According to Mr. and Mrs. Ruiz (Shelby's parents), if you slip up on one test or get a B in one class, you "break the chain" and therefore won't get a scholarship to go to a really excellent college. So Shelby, who is kind of tensed out already from the gymnastics, gets even *more* wound up and it stops her from enjoying stuff like summer and hanging out on the beach (mostly with me).

Shelby's parents knew their plan wouldn't sit well with me or the rest of the Outriders, so they added the extra-harsh warning that if Shelby flaked on even one day of summer school they would send her off to one of those boarding schools where you live in a dormitory. I told Shelby they were bluffing because they didn't have the cash to send her to one of those schools, but Shelby told me her dad threatened to "sell the house" or do "whatever it takes" for her to get a better education. That's how extra-harsh and evil these people were. So you see, Tremendous Problem Number One was that at the very moment that plankton was bioluminescent-ing and glowing blue inside the cave, Shelby was stuck going to summer school and if she ditched, we would lose her forever.

TREMENDOUS PROBLEM NUMBER TWO:

We didn't know we would find two robbers at Blue Cave who would eventually kidnap Shelby's little sister Annabelle.

But I'll get to all that stuff later.